Liverpool

A Tale of Three Cities

Lilipool

Table of Contents

Dedication

For you, Mum, God bless.

And Jean-Pierre, for the good times

About the Author

The author, Linda Mathis, aka Lilipool, born in England, lives in Southern France, between the sea and mountains, surrounded by vineyards.

Her career spans four decades, mainly in international and multinational firms around the world.

Linda Mathis is a mother of two grown-up sons and now spends the majority of her time writing and painting.

Chapter One

THE WEDGING

You've made your bed; now you must lie in it. Lili thought once again, but this time there was no getting away from it. This was her honeymoon, her first night as Madame Beaumont!

Accommodated in the bridal suite of the Royal Crown Hotel overlooking Lake Windermere in the English Lake District, known as The Lakes. The breathtaking beauty of the area, situated between North West England and Scotland, was well worth the long journey in their small Lotus Elan sports car. It was chockablock full of their two small suitcases and toilet bags for their fifteen-day honeymoon, touring the Lakes and Scotland. "Just married" was sprayed all over the bonnet with multi-coloured ribbons blowing in the breeze. The broomsticks and all the other paraphernalia had fallen off long ago on the drive up North on the M6 motorway.

The awful truth hit her, Anthony, her groom, was in love with another man, his best friend, Paul, now on a three-year assignment with his firm in the States. Paul had telephoned at the end of the wedding feast in the romantic Italian restaurant in Lower Bridge Street, Chester, to wish the couple good luck and apologise again he could not be there in the role of Best Man. He was on holiday sailing off Cape Cod in Massachusetts with Kate, the lovely ivory-skin beauty from the French Embassy, who he had recently met and with whom he was already very smitten. He compared her beauty to Titian's painting 'Venus of Urbino'. Anthony was totally irritated and very glad the conversation ended when the connection was suddenly cut off.

Prior to Paul's phone call, while happily entering the restaurant, arm in arm with Anthony and smiling, Lili looked truly gorgeous, like all brides on their wedding day, in her long three-layer white silk dress and wide-brimmed white hat covering the right side of her face, a familiar song was playing in the background that suddenly brought happy tears to her eyes. It was the song "A Whiter Shade of Pale" by the group Procol Harum; *of course*, she thought, nobody else would think of playing that at my wedding other than Rod, a brother of mine.

Rod was standing behind the bar with a wide grin on his face from ear to ear. Lili and Rod were close siblings; just a nod, a wink, or a smile, and they understood what the other was thinking or feeling. They had spent many nights together, lost youth, in front of the big fireplace in Rod's flat in Chester, drinking and listening to Leonard Cohen's records and putting the world to right.

"Rod, only you could know how much I love this Procol Harum song and how much I wanted it played on my wedding day. You being in Chester for my wedding with your new thick beard came as such a surprise when I saw you yesterday. You should still be traveling around Europe on your bike, but you said you couldn't miss my wedding for anything, and you peddled back fast enough to be here in time. Bless you; you'll definitely go to heaven, but not just yet; let's dance together to this amazing music."

After clearing the tables and the hilarious speech by Igor, the Best Man, both in English and French, following the traditional cutting of the cake by the bride and groom, Igor suddenly stood up as straight as a rod, arms at his sides and at the top of his voice started singing the French national anthem – *La Marseillaise*.

Anthony got up and joined in, very surprised. His brothers and the rest of the French guests followed suit. It was a splendid moment, never to be forgotten. It had been a sumptuous wedding feast and a good gathering of the two Clans.

Anthony left shortly after singing *La Marseillaise*. He wanted to drive straight away up to The Lakes for the honeymoon. Even to the detriment of his close family, who had made the long journey from France, as well as their friends who had come from all corners of the globe to attend their wedding. He just stood up and left and told Lili to get in the car. She so wanted to stay, to sing, dance, drink champagne and have fun with their thirty-two guests, including Pauline, her friend from London, who was expecting a baby a week before Lili's birthday in October. Lili was delighted to be one of the future Godmothers.

Lili swore to herself she'd never tell anyone the marriage had not been consummated on their wedding night. Embarrassed and bitterly hurt, she only had herself to blame. After all, she had already guessed the truth. She was wondering where the future would lead; only time would tell.

Lili was attracted to Anthony the first fateful evening they met in Paris. Tall, slim, straight blond hair, stylishly too long over his shirt collar, and those wide green eyes, dark as a moonless mountaintop at night. Casually but smartly dressed, the way only the French know-how, with a little mischievous air about him, and undoubtedly intelligent in an academic sense. Unlike Lili, who had street-wise intelligence, you could rarely pull the wool over her eyes, Lili knew.

He somehow and unfathomably brought out her maternal instincts, the ones she didn't know she had.

Chapter Two
GROWING UP IN LIVERPOOL

Lili had never behaved like a child, always acting like a little mother. She was brought up in the City of Liverpool by her Liverpudlian mother, Elsa-May, now a divorced woman with four children. Each child was born in Liverpool about two years apart. Her husband LJ, their father, had left when he met Deidra, an attractive brunette who owned a grocery shop in Birkenhead on the other side of the river Mersey and had a bit of money when she became a widow a short time before she and LJ became lovers.

LJ was remarkably handsome and of second-generation Irish descent. He had obviously rubbed the blarney stone many times. He could turn on his charms when he knew there would be something worthwhile in it for him. Not the type to stay at home with wife and kids in the evening, but the type who prefers to go out every night drinking beer and whisky, play snooker and bet with his fellow Liverpudlians in the local Pubs and Alehouses. Yes, LJ enjoyed a bevvy.

They practically never saw their father, and when they did, they rarely or never spoke. Lili simply couldn't remember if they had ever spent a Christmas, Easter, a birthday, or any kind of event together as a family.

LJ loved watching boxing matches, the ones with the Marquess of Queensberry rules, and never missed a match in the city centre on Friday nights. He was a good boxer himself, in great shape. He used to take Elsa-May to the matches during their whirlwind courtship, but nowadays, she stayed home with the children and cooked the best Scouse dinners in the whole of Liverpool. They loved Scouse, a typical Liverpudlian dish, which is a sort of stew made from either lamb or beef from Sunday's leftovers and winter vegetables.

Elsa-May played the piano well, mostly jazz but also some classics. Her favourite music was boogie-woogie. Her long slim fingers moved wildly over the keys, and she could play it as good as she could dance it. She and LJ had made a very handsome couple; everyone said so. Elsa-May loved music and dancing, but not with LJ. However, he did sing often and had a good voice, and loved to listen to vinyl records or the radio. LJ had two left feet, according to Elsa-May, and danced with her as if he were driving a truck.

Her ever-so-sweet mother-in-law told Elsa-May about LJ's bravery during WW2. He was a war hero and received many medals, especially for fighting the Japanese in the

Burma jungle. He was one of the forgotten British soldiers, still fighting after the declaration of peace because nobody could get inside the jungle to tell them the war was over for five long years and the Allied forces had won, and the ruthless Dictator, Adolf Hitler, had died in his bunker in Germany.

Lili's teenage years began at the start of the Swinging 60's era with The Beatles, also known as The Fab 4: John Lennon, Paul McCartney, George Harrison, and Ringo Starr, who made up the Liverpool rock band. They played at the Cavern Club and were her dreamboats, her idols. Lili would get on the bus in front of her house and go into the centre of Liverpool to The Cavern Club to watch and hear them sing. They were part of the *Mersey Sound*, which was bands and singers like The Beatles, Gerry, and the Pacemakers, Rory Storm & The Hurricanes, The Remo Four, and Johnny Sandon & The Searchers, to name but a few, who were part of that special Mersey sound.

The City of Liverpool, the fifth largest Metropolitan area in the United Kingdom and the third largest seaport, is situated at the mouth of the river Mersey as it meets the Irish Sea in North West England. It was a small fishing port until the late 17th century, when it experienced rapid growth thanks to the expansion of the British Empire into the trade colonies of North America and the West Indies. This explained why the music was called the "Mersey Sound", named after the Mersey River.

Of the four Beatles, Lili had no physical preference but preferred John Lennon's voice. She could sing any of The Beatles' songs off by heart; in fact, Lili was always singing. If she wasn't singing, she was playing sports and games or being the little mother to her siblings. She was the eldest girl of Elsa-May's four children...boy, girl, boy, girl.

This kept Lili slim and athletic looking with her light brown hair and natural auburn streaks, cut and styled in a bob. People said she was outgoing and fearless. Actually, she was reserved and could never hide her feelings due to her big blue eyes, they told it all, and she often blushed when receiving compliments. Elsa-May used to say anyone could read Lili like an open book.

"Lili, come downstairs for your dinner and stop making that racket throwing darts at the Tina Moore poster hanging in your bedroom. The neighbours will start complaining again; I've had enough, and I'm sick of it."

Lili didn't care what her mother said; she was jealous and had a big crush on Tina's husband, Bobby Moore, the Captain of England's football team that won the FIFA World

Cup in 1966 by a score of 4-2 at Wembley Stadium against West Germany.

She knew Bobby Moore was ten years her senior, and she didn't have a hope in hell of ever meeting him, let alone going out with him. Still, Bobby Moore was considered the best centre-back in football history. He was handsome, modest, and talented. Lili's two brothers were at the winning final on the 30th of July, 1966, in Wembley Stadium, London. Lili considered them to be very lucky blighters, indeed.

The whole of the United Kingdom was happy, deliriously happy. The cup was won by Alf Ramsey's 'wingless wonders team' as all the press and newspapers described the new tactical way the team played. England's one and only FIFA World Cup win, thanks to their inspirational Captain, Bobby Moore, and also to Geoff Hurst's hat-trick. What a team: Alan Ball, Gordon Banks, Bobby Charlton, Jacky Charlton, George Cohen, Roger Hunt, Geoff Hurst, Martin Peters, Bobby Moore, Nobby Stiles, and Ray Wilson; what a game, what memories, and what glorious world champions.

Lili was very proud of being British, born in Liverpool, England, and to be a Liverpool lass, lass being the name given to girls and young women in the North of England.

Chapter Three
THE PARIS TRIP

Ivy, eighteen years old, Lili's younger sister by nearly five years, as lovely as the sun shining on a wheat field on a summer's day, with long blonde wavy hair and legs that went all the way up to her bottom, accompanied Lili to Paris on a weekend trip in August while Lili's live-in boyfriend, Jay, was working abroad, in Philadelphia, for a couple of months with his first new client. It had been Jay's idea.

Over the phone from across the Atlantic Ocean, Jay had said:

"Lili, get out of the city, get out of our flat in London, it's so hot and stifling at this time of year, go and visit some places, perhaps with your sister Ivy. Take some time off work, don't hang around and mope, I've got work that must be done, but that shouldn't stop you from taking off. Use some of the money in the joint account."

"All right, that's it then, I will."

Lili, aka the bulldozer, is never one to let the grass grow under her feet and not afraid to go where angels fear to tread, there and then put a plan into action to visit gay Paris. She had never been to France but had always fancied the idea of visiting Paris, its capital city.

Lili phoned Ivy, now living with their mother and two brothers in the wonderful Roman City of Chester in the North West of England, some 30 miles from Liverpool. It was the house where Lili herself used to live, within the old Roman city walls with the largest Roman Amphitheatre in Great Britain, the oldest existing racecourse called Roodee, Saint Werburgh's English gothic style cathedral, the Dee River meandering through the city with pleasure boats for rides to the Weir rapids. She asked Ivy if she was free to accompany her to Paris for a few days and, moreover, if the idea appealed to her.

"Yeah, you're kidding; you're pulling my leg, right? You're barmy, completely nuts. I'm definitely up for it, especially if you're paying because I'm skint; I still haven't found THE job or any job. Nowadays, companies only seem to be hiring Graduates, those with university degrees."

"I can't figure out why you always managed to find good jobs. You handed in your notice on Friday and started a new job on Monday. Actually, I'm going to apply to the Police Force to see if there are any opportunities, but, yeah, Lili, sure, I can apply when we get back, and I'll bet Mum won't mind."

Lili knew that Elsa-May would not mind or oppose; on the contrary, she loved to see the sisters spend time together, which wasn't often since Lili moved to London with cousin Jen.

Without much more ado, Ivy arrived with her small red suitcase on two wheels a few days later at Euston railway station in London. Together, the sisters, arm in arm, flew to Paris-Orly from London-Heathrow. Up, up and away.

Chapter Four
THE GUT FEELING

As soon as they arrived in Paris, Lili didn't know or understand what had hit her or what was happening. While she was strolling around the boulevards and avenues of Paris, she just knew without any doubt that Paris was the place where she must live for the rest of her life to give it purpose and grow roots; she had a gut feeling.

"Always listen to your gut feeling; the gut feeling never lies; go where your heart takes you, and look for the signs."

That was what her Gran always said. Gran was her mother's mother and also the person who told Lili one day when she was a young kid.

"Lili, if you see a Catholic coming towards you, cross over the street to the other side."

"But Gran, how will I know if the person is Catholic, Protestant, or whatever?"

"You'll just know; you'll have the gut feeling."

Gran was a true 'Orange', The Dutchman, King William III, widely known as William of Orange or King Billy, the Protestant, married to Mary II, became King of England, Ireland & Scotland, ruling jointly with his wife from 1689, after the 'Glorious Revolution', meaning without any bloodshed. He was Gran's hero. The whole family participated in the Orange Lodge Parade through Liverpool every year on July 12th.

There were no good Catholics, according to Gran. Lili couldn't and never would understand or adhere to that racist way of thinking.

Unfortunately, this remained true of Gran, even after her own death, when she disinherited her eldest daughter Elsa-May in her Will because she had married a Catholic. It was her youngest daughter Dorothy who inherited it all. Sadly, she never shared a penny, a trinket, or a photo with her one and only sibling, Elsa-May, who was terribly hurt, never ever got over the betrayals of both her mother and only sister.

Not that Gran disliked the four grandchildren who were the fruits of that Catholic marriage, she loved them to bits.

Anytime one of them came to visit, especially Lili, there would always be a sausage in the frying pan and a plate of chips to eat, and a glass of pop to drink, which was mostly sarsaparilla, later named cola.

"Take your coat off and pour the tea while I heat up the sausages and put the chip pan on. Chas, you poke the fire and put some more coal on."

Gran said that to her longtime lover, the one the kids called Uncle Chas. The man Gran had taken in after the war when her husband, their maternal grandfather, had gone off to live and begin a new life with another woman, one he'd met from the Women's Royal Air Force (WRAFs).

Uncle Chas was Welsh. He sang like a lark and never spoke much, a man of very few words, but he didn't need to speak; he was kind, gentle, and nice. He drove a bin lorry and often said:

"You know, there's a lot of money to be made in muck."

It was certainly true because they lived well in their terrace house in Bootle; one of Liverpool's suburbs, kept up with the Joneses, had all the latest gadgets, and spent each summer holidaying in a luxury caravan in South Wales where Uncle Chas was born. Gran was basically a good person, one of the best, and they were the best. Nobody could deny that.

Chapter Five

THE FRENCH ENCOUNTER

The signs were definitely there, everywhere; Paris was magic, infatuating, invigorating. Inebriating.

While crossing the rue Claire in the area of the Ecole Militaire on the left bank, where they shared a twin-bedded room in a cosy two-star hotel, Lili and Ivy nearly got run over by a red car driven very fast.

"Can you believe it, bloody French gits? He's a stupid divvy driver!"

Lili shouted after the Peugeot 504 convertible car that hurtled down the street; she gave it the middle finger sign and used the F word. Then suddenly, with a screech of brakes, the car turned around and passed close to them, the car's passenger held up a computer punch card with a smiley picture drawn on it marked "Un pot ce soir? - a drink this evening?"

How Lili and Ivy laughed, holding on to each other, falling about the pavement, saying:

"Only the French could be so bold, cheeky, inimitable, and so 'je ne sais quoi' as the phrase book said ha-ha."

They were both very hungry and excited about the idea of eating real French food in the small Bistro on the corner of a nearby street, the first one they had spotted upon arriving at the hotel. Neither of them could speak French. Fathoming out what to choose from the long list on the menu was proving to be a challenge.

Suddenly, two young men came and sat next to them. In perfect English with an unmistakable French accent, they asked if they could be of any help with the menu.

"What! It was you two who tried to run us over a few minutes ago; you nearly killed us, you treated us like bowling pins, you were going for a strike, you must be joking, no, off with you."

But they all laughed, and a friendship that would change the course of Lili's life forever began that hot summer evening with Anthony in Paris, where things happen.

At eight o'clock, they were eating duck foie gras on lightly toasted baguette bread with fig chutney, chosen by Paul, Anthony's friend, colleague, and driver, which Lili called pâté, but she was taken to task by Anthony, who told her she was ignorant

"Foie gras is a famous French duck liver delicacy, not to be compared to a vulgar pâté."

An escalope of veal followed the foie gras with Morilles mushrooms in a cream sauce. Lili was licking her lips and feeling very chuffed; her Morilles mushrooms, shaped like small bells, had a very subtle, delicate taste.

"I could get used to eating like this, but I'd gain a kilo every day."

Not likely Ivy, Lili thought; Ivy only weighed 55 kilos and was 1.70 metres tall.

Paul couldn't take his eyes off Ivy. He had no appetite; he just drank some good red wine he'd chosen from the Bordeaux region and grinned. He looked into Ivy's blue eyes as if he were drowning in the Pacific Ocean. Anthony did all the talking, and when they couldn't eat anything more, the Frenchmen paid the bill without batting an eyelid.

The sisters were getting tired; it had been a hard day's night, travelling, sightseeing, wining, and dining; they now wanted to go to bed to start being tourists early the next day. However, Paul would not hear of it. He insisted on showing them Paris-by-night. He was very persuasive, not taking no for an answer. In all fairness, Paul proved to be an entertaining and knowledgeable guide.

Close to the Bistro, where they had just eaten in the 7th arrondissement, their guided tour began at the Ecole Militaire, an impressive complex of buildings in the Military

Institution, founded in 1750 by King Louis XV (b.1710-d.1774) of the House of Bourbon dynasty. The only French King who had been born and died in the Château de Versailles.

He was nicknamed "Louis le bien aimé" – Louis the well-loved – however, he was a notorious womaniser; his favourite mistress was La Marquise de Pompadour, aka Madame de Pompadour, a very refined and beautiful woman with exquisite taste, talented in the arts and an influential member of the French Bourgeoisie.

Motoring down the Avenue des Invalides, where the splendid Hôtel des Invalides stood. Built in 1670 by King Louis XIV (b.1638-d.1715) to accommodate and nurse the invalids of his numerous armies during his many wars. Louis XIV, also known as "Louis le Grand" – Louis the Great - and "The Sun King" because wherever he was King, the sun shinned. He was King in the Americas and in Europe. The reign of Louis XIV lasted for 72 years, longer than that of any other European sovereign, then and today.

Lili, a great Beatles fan, had read that John Lennon was inspired by King Louis XIV to write the song "Sun King", which is on the Abbey Road album launched in 1969. Such lovely melodious music and lyrics.

The Hôtel des Invalides is also where the self-proclaimed Emperor, the Corsican, Napoléon Bonaparte – Napoléon Premier, lies in the great tomb. Born in Ajaccio in 1769, died in 1821 on the island of Sainte-Hélène. The Invalides' golden dome lit up the sky, so majestic, so regal. The sisters decided they must visit it at length one day.

Driving over the Pont d'Alma – where Lady Diana, Princess of Wales, would die many years later on the 31st of August, 1997, as a result of sustained injuries caused in a tragic car accident while trying to escape the cameras of the French paparazzi, they arrived on the Avenue des Champs-Elysées, the world's most beautiful tree-lined avenue. To actually be there, driving up towards the Arc de Triomphe, with the big French red, white and blue flag flying in the middle of the Arc, simply said it all.

They pinched each other to remind themselves where they were and realised their true luck to be in Paris.

"I feel sorry for anyone who's not us tonight." Ivy said.

They circled around the Arc de Triomphe at the top of the Avenue des Champs-Elysées, also known as the Place de l'Etoile – meaning star – because of the twelve avenues leading off it. Paul parked the car in one of the avenues and invited Lili and Ivy for a nightcap at the famously refined

Fouquet's restaurant and lounge bar located on the corner of the Avenue des Champs-Elysées and the Avenue George V.

The Avenue George V is a landmark in Paris, named after the United Kingdom's King George V, the first Monarch of today's House of Windsor dynasty.

He was the father of the brave, stuttering King George VI who helped spur the Allied Forces to victory with Sir Winston Churchill against Adolph Hitler and Nazi Germany during WW2.

King George VI became King despite all odds, following the abdication of his wretched brother, King Edward VIII, who fratanised with the Germans and didn't care a fig about his British Subjects. He abdicated to be able to marry the divorced American socialite, Mrs. Wallis Simpson, because the Government would not allow him to marry a divorced woman. The couple later became The Duke and Duchess of Windsor and made their home in the suburbs of Paris.

Settled in the plush red armchairs in Fouquet's, Paul insisted they order a bottle of champagne and drink in honour of the sisters' first trip to Paris. He made a toast to:

"Les jolies demoiselles de Liverpool - the pretty young women from Liverpool."

Paul invited them to eat at his apartment in the 15ième arrondissement - the 15th District - the next day, which was already the next day.

Instantly Ivy declined, saying how nice the invitation was and how much they appreciated it, but she and Lili had a long schedule of visits planned, including the Eiffel Tower and Notre Dame de Paris Cathedral.

Ivy was not in the least bit attracted to Paul. Despite his chivalrous ways and pleasant voice, he simply wasn't her type; he was just too old for her. He was a younger blond version of Maurice Chevalier, but without the straw hat. She preferred tall, dark-skinned, dark-haired, heavy-built, down-to-earth men who liked to share a good laugh and joke, drink pints of beer, play snooker and watch football.

Unfortunately, Paul, not about to give in easily, accepted they wouldn't eat at his place but announced he and Anthony would pick them up at their hotel on rue Claire at nine o'clock and continue the guided tour by-day this time.

After being escorted back to their hotel and lying on the beds in their room after showering, Ivy piped-up

"To hell with Paul; we've come to Paris to have a giggle and be together. I feel like we're being herded around like lost sheep. Heaven knows we're more than capable of reading a metro map and finding our way about. I know we don't want to hurt Paul's feelings because they did pay for our dinner, which probably cost an arm and a leg. The sightseeing ride after dinner was fun in the gorgeous red Peugeot convertible. It was great to be sitting inside looking up at the sites out of the open-top roof, but frankly, I find him pushy and intrusive."

"Yeah, you're right, Luv, I have similar reservations myself, but I do like Anthony. I like the way it's easy to talk to him and the way he looks away shyly when he smiles. I feel he's definitely not running after me; I've no need to be afraid he'll want to get into my knickers. But, just to be on the safe side for tomorrow, look in the French phrase-book to find out how to say 'sod off, get your hand off my knee'."

They giggled again in the dark.

"Let's get some kip; it's late. I want to buy some croissants and fresh baguette bread from the Boulangerie next door as soon as we get up and dress to eat on a bench before taking the metro."

They soon fell into a deep sleep.

Up with the alarm at half-passed seven, they had a cat's lick and dressed in light blue jeans and printed short-sleeved off-the-shoulder cotton tops and flat-heeled shoes. Casual clothes to mingle as tourists. It was mid-August and very hot. *Even if she wore a potato sack on her back, Ivy would make it look lovely,* Lili thought while gazing admiringly at her younger sister.

Patting themselves on the back and thinking how clever they were by getting up early to be far away from the hotel when Paul and Anthony were supposed to be at the reception desk at nine o'clock. They were super surprised when the lift door opened downstairs, and they saw the duet already there, sitting at one of the dining tables with a full Continental breakfast ordered and served.

Well, bugger me, thought Lili, feeling light-headed.

Following much discussion, they ate the delicious breakfast, and it was decided Paul, accompanied by Anthony, would drive the sisters wherever they wanted to go during the day. They never did get to ride on the metro.

Ivy made it very clear that after the days' visits, she and Lili would eat together, probably in the Latin Quarter by the River Seine near Notre-Dame de Paris Cathedral, where there are lots of students and young people. They'd been told by the hotel receptionist that in the Latin Quarter, there was a very large choice of restaurants with every type of food imaginable from all over the world to accommodate everyone's taste and budget.

Lili was pleasantly surprised by how much attention Anthony paid her and how much they laughed at and about the same things. However, she could see Ivy was getting cheesed-off by the advances Paul was making to her. Especially when they were on the second floor of the Eiffel Tower, which is known as the world's biggest phallic symbol, looking towards the fountains at the Trocadero and the Palais de Chaillot, when Paul put his arm around Ivy's waist, pointing to show her a boat the French call a bateau mouche – fly boat – sailing on the Seine passing just in front of the Tower, Ivy became very irate and flipped.

"OK, everyone," Ivy said between clenched teeth, "it's time to get the elevator down and back to our hotel, Lili and I need to rest and change our clothes before going to dinner unless you want to walk down the 674 steps."

Later, back in the hotel room, Ivy let off some steam again

"That's it, I won't see them anymore, Paul thinks he's a lady-killer, but I've got news for him. If you want to keep seeing Anthony, it's up to you; it's your shout. But not for me. Now, let's look at the bus map again to see how we can get to the Latin Quarter and have a walk along the Seine before dinner. I'm dying to get on one of the old buses we've seen, the ones where we can stand outside on the deck at the back."

It was a warm and pleasant evening. They really enjoyed crossing Paris on that old bus, which certainly cheered Ivy up. They got off at the Saint-Michel Fountain and walked along the Quay de la Tournelle by the side of the river opposite the magnificent gothic cathedral. Along the river, they saw lots of Bateaux mouches boats passing, people having picnics sitting on coloured tablecloths on the cobbled stones lining the river, lovers walking holding hands, and accordion music being played all around them.

While strolling and talking, Lili and Ivy became famished, especially as they hadn't eaten anything since the surprise breakfast, and it was now late evening.

Mingling through the very narrow streets of the Latin Quarter with tourists and Parisians who hadn't yet left Paris on holiday, there were at least a hundred restaurants, and the aromas and smells made their mouths water. They chose a Greek restaurant that had whole fresh fish, meat on skewers, and big red peppers displayed inside the large open window. As they sipped the cold white wine and ate the marvelous Mediterranean food, they exchanged conversations with other customers sitting at the nearby tables. It was divine and fun; they had pleasant anecdotes to share during the taxi ride back to the hotel.

To their great surprise, Anthony was waiting, browsing through some brochures, at the hotel reception when they returned. He jumped up, saying he wanted to say "au revoir" before they returned to London the following afternoon. Ivy coughed and looked grumpy. She excused herself and went up to their room.

Anthony was a bit shy, looking at his fingernails and fidgeting. He said Paul was sorry Ivy was evidently not attracted to him and that she paid him little or no attention, but he had encouraged Anthony to see Lili again because they both liked her.

Lili explained again that she had a live-in boyfriend in London named Jay and this trip to Paris was to bide time until his return from business abroad. Anthony shooed the subject aside as if he hadn't heard a word.

"Actually, I came to give you this Essay written by Stéphane Hessel called 'Indignez-vous' it's the translated version – 'Get angry! Cry out'. Hessel is a person I admire greatly. In addition to everything he writes in the Essay and all the food he gives us for thought, he was one of the Statesmen who oversaw the writing of the "Universal Declaration of Human Rights" before its signature in 1948 in the "Musée de l'Homme" inside the Palais de Chaillot, the building we saw today from the Eiffel Tower, on the other side of the Seine."

"Lili, I like you a lot, I haven't had many girlfriends, and Paul is my only friend in Paris. We work together in a big corporation, and we share the commuting; he drives us there one week, and I drive the next. It's less boring, saves money, and the journey seems somehow shorter. We often go out together after work. There's something about you I admire that attracts me, even in the short time I've known you. I can talk to you easily, and I enjoy our discussions; that's why I know you'll appreciate the Stéphane Hessel Essay. He says never to be complacent about any situation, and if something revolts you, you should cry out, shout out, and protest. I can see you're that type. I miss you already, Lili, and you haven't left Paris yet, isn't that strange?"

"Lili, why don't you come back again next weekend or the one after? Ivy won't be here and neither will Paul, he's going on a trip to the Côte d'Azur - The French Riviera -, so there will only be the two of us."

Lili was taken aback by the way he said it in his romantic French accent. His English was nearly perfect. He said his English was good thanks to his English teacher in college. The teacher loved the English and their culture to such an extent he was able to transmit his passion of the language to his students.

Suddenly, troubled, she realised how the stories about Frenchmen were true, the way they flirted and had such eloquence.

While being in Anthony's company, memories of Jay, her first love, came flooding back into her mind, remembering he was her only love, her love at first sight experience, the man she was actually living with in their smart second-floor flat in a big Victorian house in West London that she had found after much searching and which they had decorated and furnished together.

She was thinking about how her relationship with Jay was currently going down the drain. She was feeling lost, not knowing what to do about it, how to fix it, or how to move forward. The fact he was working abroad again for a while, this time for himself, didn't make the situation easier. She really needed to talk things over with him and explain how lonely she was feeling; he treated her like part of the furniture. She needed to get it off her chest and make some decisions; she didn't want things to go on indefinitely the way they were. Life was too short; she didn't want to be taken for granted, and she wanted to live her dreams, of which she had many.

Lili grudgingly thought if Jay wasn't working long and late hours, he was training, playing, or watching rugby; he was a fanatic. He also suffered from some form of psychosomatic illness, lack of confidence, frustration, headaches, and nausea even when they went on holiday, which was quite often. They visited many different European and Scandinavian countries. However, recently, he was no longer himself, the man she loved; he was distant. She sensed there wasn't much space left in Jay's life for her anymore.

Chapter Six

LOVE AT FIRST SIGHT

Lili's train of thought went back, remembering when they were both nineteen years old; she and her cousin Jen were invited to a party on a Saturday night in a big house in Southport, a seaside town near Liverpool, shared by six co-workers from Jen's team. The music and the ambience were great; everyone knew each other, and laughter could be heard throughout the house.

When Lili went into the kitchen to get some food from the buffet, she stopped in her tracks. There was a tall, dark-haired, brown-eyed man about twenty-seven years old, casually dressed in dark grey jeans and a white polo-necked sweater. He was with another girl, pretty and petite, his arm possessively wrapped around her neck. Lili couldn't stop starring, looking, watching, mouth open. Jen came along and gave her a shove.

"Are you all right, Luv? What's up with you?"

"Yeah, I think so. I don't really know. Who's that good-looking bloke talking to that pretty girl over there?"

"Oh, that's Jay; he's in I/T and usually keeps himself to himself, but he has a way with the girls."

"With me, too, I've got wobbly knees."

The party continued until the early hours; Lili lost sight of Jay in the crowded rooms. She couldn't get him off her mind.

A couple of months passed, when one afternoon, Jen phoned Lili from her office in Liverpool, saying they were both invited again to another party at the same house in Southport and asked if she could get the train from Chester for them to go together. Lili replied affirmatively and hoped and prayed Jay would be there.

She was drinking a beer near the record-player while choosing some records to put on when she felt a hand on her back. She turned around, it was Jay, and she was totally flabbergasted.

"Hello, try to find a Rolling Stones album, preferably Beggars Banquet. I feel like bopping around the room, perhaps with you, if you're up for it."

She loved his deep voice and smooth, easy approach. He was alone this time. They stayed together, just the two of them, the whole time. They danced, drank some beers, and talked; it was wonderful!

Time flew by; it was already the early hours of the morning, the sun was rising, and it was dawn. Those who were not sleeping on the sofas or on the floor, including Jen, made some omelettes and drank fresh orange juice and mugs of tea and coffee.

In his deep sexy voice, Jay asked if he could give the girls a lift home. Lili had said she was staying over at Jen's house near Aintree racecourse, where the world-famous Grand National Steeplechase takes place once every year. He was heading off, saying he had some important stuff to get done before Monday.

Lili lived on cloud 9 after THE kiss when he dropped them off at Jen's house. She thought about Jay day and night. She couldn't eat a thing or concentrate on her work at the Magazine. Jay had asked for her phone number, and she waited around the clock for his call. Out of the blue, one evening weeks later, when she was about to give up all hope, Jay finally called.

"Sorry I haven't been in touch, Lili, but I had commitments, a deadline at work, plus some mechanical work to do on the clutch of my car, but if you're free on Thursday night, I'd like to drive over to Chester, that's where you live with your family if I remember correctly, to take you out to dinner, you could choose the restaurant."

The rest was history. Lili was already deeply in love and crazy about Jay. Winter and spring passed, and they saw each other more and more. He was her 'Pygmalion' - they went everywhere together; he taught her so much about wines, food, restaurants, travel, politics, geography, history, fashion, and the arts. Jay was so interesting and so knowledgeable. He was a graduate and had seen and done so much; had already travelled halfway around the world.

They made love in his modern detached rented house in Liverpool. Lili gave herself to him completely; she felt loved. He was her first love, and she thought he would be the first and the last. It would be impossible to love anyone more or better. Jay was perfect, they read each other's bodies like sheet music, and the pleasure was sometimes unbearable, but they cried out for more. He told her she was very lovely, natural and funny. Once he said he loved her.

Her world came tumbling down one Sunday afternoon. Settled comfortably in Jay's house with her head on his lap on the sofa, reading the newspapers, wearing her new yellow hot pants, after a delicious lunch they'd prepared together from a recipe of beef and red peppers with brown rice, Jay announced in a low sad voice that he was going away.

"I have something to tell you, Lili. It's not easy, especially the way I feel about you. I wanted to wait until I was certain of getting this new job because it's a huge promotion for me with a big fat salary. I'm in a real rut at my current job, and the salary is lousy. I got the contract on Friday morning in the post. I have to leave England in four weeks, for at least six months, to go to Philadelphia to train, learn a new programme and be nominated as the manager of a new start-up based in London, which is owned by the Philadelphia outfit."

Lili had never been to London or flown in an aeroplane.

She was devastated, completely overwhelmed. Tears flooded her blue eyes; she clung to Jay's neck, crying and kissing his face, whispering his name over and over, asking him not to go.

"Please don't leave, please don't go, I won't be able to stand it, I'll miss you more than you could ever imagine, and you'll never come back here again, you'll be living in London, 200 miles away, I simply couldn't bear it."

But it was to be. Jay left. He wrote to Lili when he was settled-in. The hotel the company had booked for him was fine and only a ten-minute drive to work. He was on the learning curve and meeting people, and going out. He'd rented a Ford Mustang car and loved V8 engines. He was happy to be back in the USA.

Lili was miserable. Planet Earth had stopped rotating; she wanted to get off. It was a permanent blackout in her life, like living on the dark side of the moon. She looked and felt like a bag of dead mice. She didn't go out after work or at weekends; she just moped.

"How many rivers can a girl cry? I've cried too many over Jay."

On many occasions, Elsa-May and Ivy listened to her complaints and sorrows, as did cousin Jen when they talked over the phone.

"I've got to get away from here, get out of this place and change my life. I know that change is hard at first, and it gets complicated in the middle, but it could be worth it in the end. I want to believe it and get going."

Since Jay's departure, Lili had been in contact with some Employment Agencies in London to find work. One big agency told her to get to London and pass-by for an interview, they had vacancies, and one was at a well-known firm located near Piccadilly Circus that could be just up her street.

She phoned Jen to test the waters to see if she wanted a change, too, to go together to London. Surprisingly, Jen had big news. Her employer in Liverpool had asked if she would be interested in transferring to the London branch to help handle logistics. They needed extra staff with experience and would give her a raise; pay her travel expenses as well as her first month's accommodation in a place that HR would find.

Jen was interested but didn't want to go to London alone. Lili cheered,

"Well, what about that for a coincidence and a great piece of luck and good news! I think it's fate; we're meant to go to London together, let's do it, let's go in two weeks' time. I have to give a week's notice to my boss at the Magazine and get my things sorted."

Lili and her cousin Jen always got on like a house on fire. They had been inseparable since childhood, like twins. They were the same age and always went everywhere together. Her sister Ivy would never admit it, even to herself, but she was a bit jealous of their relationship. Cousin Jen, like Ivy, was blond, but Jen's hair was waist-length and straight. Jen was very tall, like her father and brother, and had a communicative smile and laugh with just the right amount of self-confidence.

Jen would often compare herself to 'Alice through the looking glass'. She could spend hours and hours sitting down and looking at herself in the big dressing table mirror in front of the window in the bedroom, changing her hairstyle, her make-up, dressing up, and waiting for things to happen. Lili would talk, sit and watch her. When they were younger in college, Jen said, "Lili, you're one of those people who doesn't wait for special occasions or good things to happen; you make them happen."

Things were definitely happening now and looking good for a change. Lili felt giddy with happiness and could see there was a future for her again after the separation.

Chapter Seven

THE BIG STEP – MOVING TO LONDON

Still remembering those events, back then, how she and cousin Jen moved to London two weeks after their decision to go was taken. It was early on a Saturday morning, they excitedly said good-bye to their mothers, the sisters Elsa-May and Dorothy, on the platform at Liverpool's Lime Street station. Three and a half hours later they arrived at London's Euston station on the new, very comfortable, fast and non-stop Inter-city train.

They were getting their goods and chattels off the train and looking for a porter. It was so busy; the scene was so different from anything the cousins knew. They heard the chief porter say:

"All right mate, get their gear and put it on the trolley and take them to the Taxi stand over there on the right."

"Okay, where to, Darlin'?"

They hardly understood a word; the Northern Liverpudlian accent was so different from that of the Southern Cockney accent. It was a real culture shock for the cousins. So many different nationalities and colours, people wandering and rushing around, talking fast, very fast!

"Gosh, I hope we're going to cope with this new life, leaving home, getting our own place, fending for ourselves, and above all, will you be able to get a job soon, Lili? We've got digs to live in for a month, paid for by my firm, but after that, we'll only have ourselves to count on because our families are unable to help us out financially."

Lili didn't let that get her down. She thought Jen was right; of course, Jen was starting to get cold feet, but they'd manage. The invincible duo, no turning back now, never looking behind, look straight ahead. She felt good, really good, for the first time since Jay went away.

Lili had not written to Jay about going to live in London with Jen. His letters were few and far between; he was doing fine. She had only received one phone call late at night because of the six hours time difference. She had stopped writing.

As they looked out of the taxi window during the drive to the address in West Dulwich in South London, where they were going to live together, they could see that London was definitely the 'Melting Pot' of the United Kingdom, made up of all nationalities and skin colours, The driver was friendly and kept talking to them, explaining what the different monuments were, but for all they understood he could have been speaking in Swahili or Japanese, they didn't understand his accent or a word he said.

Finally, they arrived at 8 Newbridge Street in West Dulwich. They told each other they had better get bus, train and tube maps urgently to learn how to use the public transport system. The taxi cost a small fortune and would leave a hole in their budget. They were startled. The money for the taxi fare was a gift from their mothers, but it hadn't been enough. They had four suitcases between them as well as two big bags full of pots, pans and linen. They would never have been able to get it all on a tube, train or bus.

The landlady, Mrs Allcock, was very sharp and basically uncivil. It was obvious she was only renting this one-room bed-sit in her house to help spin out her pension. She explained she was a retired civil servant. The semi-detached house with a small garden was up for sale. She was going to live with her sister in Devonshire because they were both widows and needed to help each other make ends meet.

Mrs Allcock practically read them the Riot Act; the list of things forbidden to do was as long as her arm, including no male visitors allowed on the premises. They wondered how on earth Jen's HR department had found this awful place and if they knew the rent was astronomically high, much more than it ought to be. The first month's rent had been prepaid. Mrs. Allcock made a point of saying she fully expected the following month's rent to be paid promptly in cash.

The double-size pullout sofa bed was so uncomfortable because of the springs sticking up their bums. Furthermore, it would be impossible to even swing a cat around in the tiny kitchen. They shared a bathroom and a loo with another lodger on the first floor. A nice reserved middle-aged lady called Ethel.

They laughed in the face of adversity and cried - home sweet home - nothing was going to stop them, not now, not ever, from enjoying and embracing their new life.

Unpacking was a nightmare; they had too much stuff and not enough cupboards, drawers or storage space. Deciding to leave the task until the next day, they went out to discover the suburban town. There were many pubs and a church that was having a jumble sale. The local street market was closing, but the small supermarket was still open. They bought some cold meats, tomatoes, eggs, sliced bread, butter, tea, sugar and milk. Easy items to prepare a cold meal before going out to one of the pubs, they would celebrate and be naughty, treat themselves to a beer.

The cousins were disappointed to find the train station was at a very long uphill walk from their accommodation, but they took the time-table to look for Monday's train from West Dulwich to the West End for Jen to go to the London branch office to start work and meet her new colleagues and for Lili to quickly find any suitable job.

Choose what you like doing, be good at it, and you'll never work a day in your life. With that in her mind, Lili walked into the Employment Agency on Regent Street full of hope on the following Monday morning on the dot at nine o'clock.

Lili sat down in the waiting area until one of the agents became free. The agency was busy, already six candidates in front of her, despite it being early. Lili was received and interviewed by Betty; they had already spoken over the phone two weeks prior. Lili had posted her curriculum vitae and a motivation letter for Betty's attention.

"Nice to meet you finally, Lili. I see you have good references, and your resumé states you have certificates in typing, short-hand writing, book-keeping, and accounting with experience in various sectors, including the Press. The job that's vacant, which I have in mind for you, is a firm that has some twenty-cinema theatres all over England. The vacancy is in the film booking department to assist two film bookers and the director's secretary with administrative tasks. The salary is good, especially for starters. They want the candidate to begin ASAP because they've interviewed several candidates during the past three weeks but haven't yet found the one that fits all their criteria. I've also seen on your CV that one of your hobbies is the cinema. If you're interested, I could try to arrange an interview for later today."

Lili couldn't believe her luck; she loved the cinema, absolutely adored it and was quite a cinephile. Sometimes she would leave one cinema and go directly to another one if the critics were good and the film interested her enough. Betty came off the phone.

"Yes, the director can interview you at three o'clock today. I'll register you at this agency. Here's the job description, a briefing about the firm, the name of the director, the address and, last but not least, details of the remuneration package. Good luck, and keep me informed."

Lili walked for a while along Marble Arch and Hyde Park to collect her thoughts, then had a late lunch in a coffee shop on Carnaby Street, close to where she was going for the interview. She had walked a lot; she had her wits about her and had prepared questions for the interview.

It was autumn, Lili, wearing a long-fitted dark brown velvet coat, knee-length high-heeled leather boots tied with long laces up the front, and a brown bag, arrived in the impressive building on time, feeling surprisingly confident. She presented herself at the reception and was quickly escorted to the director's office, where he was waiting for her behind a huge desk piled high with big round cans of film, celluloid, posters, photos and all sorts of junk. His name was Rob, a charmer in his early fifties, medium height and build, smoked like a trooper and made Lili feel at ease straight away. He was laid-back but asked lots of pertinent questions. He was definitely the boss. He seemed to like her, and the feeling was mutual. He introduced Lili to the other three members of the team in the big open-plan office next door, which had four desks. They greeted her warmly and tried to imitate her Liverpool accent. Lili would have to get used to that in London. Rob left the four of them to get acquainted, and the interview continued.

Two hours later, Lili was walking out through the revolving doors into the Square with a big smile on her face. Rob had offered her the job on a month's trial period as an Assistant and Trainee Film-booker to replace the one who had quit to live on the English East Coast in Yorkshire. After Rob explained the contents of the job in detail, Lili gladly accepted the offer and phoned the agency from Rob's office for the contract to be prepared and signed between them. She was to begin on Wednesday, two days later, at nine-thirty in the morning.

Before going into London for Lili's interview and Jen's first day at work, they had arranged to meet around six o'clock at the first café on entering Victoria station to travel back together on the train to their bed-sit in West Dulwich.

When they met, they both spoke at the same time in unison, so excited, so much to tell.

"You go first, Jen. I want to hear how your day went, and then I'll tell you about mine."

"It was fab; the logistics team of nine comprises five girls, including four blokes and me. Nobody is from the North; you can imagine how they love the way I behave and talk. The work is interesting and varied, but I get the feeling it's going to be stressful because our merchandise is shipped all over the UK in trucks, but there are never enough available due to a lack of drivers. Three of us had lunch together in the canteen, which is cheap and cheerful, then they showed me around the building so I could find my bearings. On Fridays, they go out together for a drink and a pizza or something. I think I'd like to join them and I can bring you along if you like. We'll soon make friends and get a social life, that's for sure."

"Wow, that sounds great, and you look much better, less stressed, and more relaxed than this morning. For my part, well, I went to the agency, and they arranged an interview this afternoon and guess what? I got a job as an Assistant and Trainee Film-booker. The firm has very smart offices in The Square near Piccadilly Circus. The Chairman's heroes are Barnum and Bailey, the circus people… The Greatest Show on Earth! I'll assist, Betty. She's the Assistant to Rob, the Boss. I'll help with the marketing and publicity for the cinemas, and correspondence with the twenty theatre managers. They put on live shows in some of the theatres and book films to show in all the theatres, renting them from Distributors such as MGM, Warner Bros and Walt Disney. The objective is to rent the best-suited films for local audiences and generate the maximum turnover for the firm. I'll often be out of the office visiting the theatres up and down the country, but when I'm here, I'll be responsible for answering the phones, directing calls, taking messages and clerking."

"I'll also work for Igor, Rob's right-arm-man and second-level hierarchy, with visioning and booking films plus administration concerning the cinema side, which I have to learn from scratch. He's great; he looks like a big bear and has a gruff laugh and a dry sense of humour. You know, very tongue in cheek. Cyril is also on the team. He's 30ish and short. He mainly books the B films, children's matinees and late-night movies, you know, the X ones. I'll obviously have to learn loads, but the salary is what I had hoped for; we'll easily be able to keep our heads above water with both our incomes."

The weeks and months whizzed by. Lili was learning the film booking trade in the theatre and cinema industry. She really enjoyed going to the Distributors' private cinemas on Wardour Street in Soho with Igor to vision the films and assist him in booking the best ones for the different types of audiences in their cinemas to maximise profits. Once Igor, as the Renter, had done the deals with the Distributors like Warner Bros., Lili typed the programmes to send off to the managers of their theatres so they could order the publicity and get ready for the start of the week, which began on Sundays.

Six months later, on a weeknight, Lili was invited to a film preview with Rob and Igor in Leicester Square. It was her first professional evening-out in a crowd.

Usually, when she arrived home in the evenings, she would read, chat, listen to the radio, and have dinner with

Jen. They didn't have a TV or a phone. Didn't want or need them. They took turns in shopping and cooking at the new flat they had found near Clapham Common, still in South London. Good riddance to Mrs. Allcock and West Dulwich. Otherwise, they'd go out with Jen's co-workers or meet-up, eat out and discover different places and districts in London before getting the tube home.

At midnight, Lili's taxi drove up in front of her address. She was glad the firm paid for transport after working hours for female staff, especially as she was tired and dying to take her high heel shoes off. Surprisingly Jen was still up, waiting for her. She was so excited, jumping up and down on the spot.

"You'll never, absolutely never believe who I had a drink with tonight at the Red Lion pub on the Common. No, let me tell you, you'll never ever guess. It was Jay, your Jay. He rang the bell an hour after I got home. I couldn't believe my eyes when I opened the door. Before I even asked him to step inside, he said he'd phoned you at your Mum's, and she told him we had moved here and she gave him our address. He's been back from Philadelphia for a month, working like a maniac, hiring staff for their new office in Wigmore Street, not too far from your building, and finding a place to live. He invited me for a drink and a bite to eat. He was surprised you weren't home and even more surprised when I told him where you were and what you do for a living. I gave him your office phone number, and he'll call you tomorrow. Oh, gosh, I hope I did the right thing!"

Lili felt weak; her head was spinning. She had to sit down and drink a glass of water. Since the move to London, she had fought a losing battle to put Jay out of her mind. She knew she was still in love with him. She had been out on a few dates, but she didn't fancy any of the men. Moreover, she couldn't stop comparing them to Jay. She was still angry that he had gone away and was disappointed he didn't keep in touch, but she hadn't made any effort either. After a bad night's sleep, tossing and turning over and over like a pancake in her bed. She got up early and went for a run on the Common. Afterwards, she took a long-time showering and dressed with care, just in case.

Towards five o'clock for the umpteenth time that day, she answered the office phone mechanically, announcing her company's name followed by her own. She nearly passed-out when she heard Jay say

"Hello, Lili, it's me!"

That unmistakable deep sexy voice made her stomach churn and her heart miss a beat.

She phoned Jen at her office to say she would be home late and not to wait up as Jay had phoned, and they arranged to meet for dinner in Covent Garden. She could hardly believe her own ears. She had butterflies in her tummy and was as nervous as a kitten walking into the restaurant. Jay was standing at the bar drinking a gin 'n' tonic and turned around the moment she walked in. He had a big smirk all over his face and picked her up and kissed her right on the mouth.

It was just like old times. Jay was so handsome, a euphemism and an understatement if ever there was one. He told her about his trip in detail, about work and getting settled in London. He was sharing a garden flat with an old university friend in Hampstead Village near the house of John Keats, the famous 18th-century English poet. It wasn't the Ritz, but he had his own big bedroom with a bathroom. Lili could only shovel food around on her plate. She couldn't eat; she just listened. He said she had changed, and she was even lovelier. He took her hand and kissed her lovingly.

She did look good, Lili felt well. She had opened a clothing account at Selfridge's store and had changed her whole wardrobe, much snazzier but casually smart. Her hair had been cut, free of charge, in the Vidal Sassoon salon on Bond Street when they were looking for models. The style really was "wash and go", so easy to manage. It was cut short all around her oval-shaped face with highlights; it made her blue eyes look even bigger, more feline.

Jay wanted her to go to his flat after dinner, but she asked him to drive her back to Clapham Common. Jen would worry, besides which, she had an early start the next day, travelling up the M1 Motorway to one of the theatres in Bedfordshire with Igor to help organise a peek preview of the new Diana Ross film about the life of Billy Holiday, the blues singer. Jay had no choice but to acquiesce, but he was peeved. He asked if they could at least spend the coming weekend together doing lazy things like going for walks on Hampstead Heath, flying a kite, cooking, listening to some music, having drinks in the King of Bohemia Pub... just like that, just walking back into her life.

As it happened, Lili had already arranged to spend that weekend with Elsa-May and Ivy at home in Chester. Her two brothers, Lee and Rod, had left home to go to university. Thankfully they agreed to meet her in Chester in the evening after their afternoon at Goodison Park supporting their team Everton FC in the local derby football match against Liverpool FC. They were ardent Evertonian fans; she crossed her fingers that Everton would win or at least draw.

Perhaps after dinner, they would go to listen to some groups at the Cross Keys Folk Club by Chester Railway Station.

Lili was catching the 6.08 pm train to Chester after work on Friday and would be back at Euston station at 9:14 pm on Sunday. She had organised the trip weeks ago and didn't want to disappoint her family by cancelling at the last minute.

Returning and getting off the Intercity train on Sunday night, walking towards the tube entrance, thinking about the good times she'd had with her family in Chester and feeling a bit home-sick already, Lili was flabbergasted to see Jay standing at the exit. He was smiling and waving and caught hold of her waist to give her a long deep kiss, and she sensed his longing.

It was bliss lying beside Jay with his arms around her in his bed in Hampstead, it was late, and she could see the moon shining through the open curtains and the shadows of the trees on the walls. They had made love with wild desire until they were both covered in each other's sweat, serene and satisfied. The separation hadn't changed a thing about the way their bodies reacted and intertwined. She had licked and caressed every inch of his body, the one she knew so well.

Curious and as mischievous as the Devil himself, Lili couldn't help herself; she questioned Jay about his time in Philadelphia, about whether he'd had any girlfriends.

"What the eyes don't see, the heart can't grieve. Lili, don't let's do this. We've been separated for seven months. Jealously doesn't suit you, and it also makes you look ugly. I didn't meet anyone like you, Lili. You're unique. Perhaps there was an older married lady hanging around me a lot, a friend's wife from work, an intellectual. She said she would write and keep in touch. That's all. I was busy, really busy, learning the ropes."

From then on, Lili and Jay became inseparable once again. Lili sometimes saw Jen for lunch during the week and went back to their flat in Clapham to spend an evening or two and to fetch some clothes. Jen had made some friends, but she also liked to stay at Hampstead sometimes on weekends with them, sleeping on the convertible sofa in the large bright living room with double French windows leading onto the garden. When Jay was playing rugby, the cousins would either go to watch the game or meet them after the match in the pub, then go to eat in the local Indian restaurant. On Sundays, they would brunch together while reading the Sunday newspapers, listen to vinyl records, drink beer at the pub and cook in the evening.

Over the years, Jen often went back at weekends to spend short holidays staying with her mother Dorothy in Liverpool. Dotty, as she was nicknamed, was lonely after Jen went to live in London with Lili. She was newly divorced from her husband Lester after a few too many spoilt Christmas dinners he threw up the walls and wrecked house decorations, amongst other things. Dotty was also depressed after the departure of Stan, her beloved eldest child, Jen's brother and Lili's cousin.

For a short period, Lili had lived with Dotty and her family in Aintree while finishing her secretarial and accounting course. In winter, she was prone to getting infected tonsils, causing septic tonsillitis. Lili had been sent home from her course one day and was so ill she didn't have the strength to walk to a doctor's surgery and couldn't speak to phone a doctor to examine her at the house. She opened her mouth wide and showed her cousin Stan her big infected tonsils; he reeled back in horror. He jumped on his motorbike and went to fetch the doctor and brought him to the house within the hour. He was a young doctor from Pakistan and wore a turban wrapped around his head. He held on to it to stop it from coming off as Stan had his foot firmly on the gas pedal and was swerving at all the corners. It was so comical to see the frightened Pakistani doctor running up the drive holding on to his turban for dear life; if she could have, Lili would have laughed hysterically. Stan was like that, funny and kind.

Stan had gone off to live and settle abroad. He would probably never leave Australia to return to Liverpool. Stan didn't like his name; he said Stan conjured-up visions of characters in the very popular British soap opera called "Coronation Street" or "Corrie" to most Northerners. Every episode was watched by millions of viewers. It was created by Granada Television and has been played on ITV since 1960. It became the most-watched programme on British independent television.

Stan preferred the name 'Caine' from David Carradine's character, Kwai Chang Caine, in the Kung-Fu Western series. Some of his mates called him Caine because they said he was a dead-ringer of the Carradine character. When he was leaving the pub, they would mock him:

"Don't go, Caine, come back."

Actors also said that in the Kung-Fu western, but Caine never came back, and neither did Stan.

Stan had taken time out before going to university. He flew from Liverpool airport to a destination in Spain with a few mates. At first, they only planned to go to Europe, but Stan got the travel bug and continued alone to Asia and then

Oceania. He was a big guy with a great sense of humour and earned good money working on building sites to pay for the next stop on his trip that didn't have a terminus. One very hot day, while working on a site in Sydney, the scaffolding on which he was standing disintegrated under his feet. He fell five stories onto the ground. He broke most of everything on his left side. His organs had been shuffled in the fall, and he had a broken skull. It was touch and go whether he would pull through. He was in dire straits.

Inevitably there was an investigation. It transpired Stan's life had been saved only because the tar covering the ground was so hot due to the summer's exceptional heatwave; it had melted and formed a soft cushion. If it had been a concrete surface, the outcome would have been entirely different.

The good thing about the terrible accident and the ordeal was that Stan fell in love with Shannon, the Ward Sister who nursed him back to life and helped him get through the numerous operations to put him back together again. He said she had the best arse in the whole of the Southern Hemisphere. He made her laugh, and she translated his broad Liverpudlian accent for all those who couldn't understand him. Two years later, when he was discharged from the hospital, with the compensation money from the insurance company, they bought a van and went exploring the wonderful Australian country for a year or two, then set-up home together on a small farm they bought with a farmhouse that had 10 acres of land. They raised sheep, pigs, and various other animals grew their own food produce and lived happily ever after.

Life down under was completely different from Liverpool's. Stan loved the open space, the mountains, the oceans and the amazing panoramas. Nevertheless, Stan missed not going to the Liverpool FC games; watching the Reds on television with a big time zone difference wasn't the same as singing 'You'll never walk alone' or 'When the Saints go marching in' at Anfield Road stadium.

During her visits to Liverpool, cousin Jen started to date Pete, a bloke she bumped into again one evening by chance. She knew him from her old college days. Their relationship was stormy but getting serious. Jen loved her job and life in London and didn't envisage going back to Liverpool, but she was seriously attracted to Pete. Unfortunately for Jen, Pete had a thing against London and Southerners in general. He just stayed once with Jen at their flat and found only negative things to say. Pete said the ball was in Jen's court. Jen decided to go back to Liverpool to give the romance a better chance of survival. Luckily, she got a good job working for one of the big insurance companies in Great Howard Street and rented a small house with Pete in Edge Hill.

After that, Lili couldn't afford to pay the rent of their flat alone and didn't want to look for a flat-mate; Jen had been the perfect one. Lili moved in with Jay in Hampstead, which wasn't an ideal situation. His flat mate Dan was often there, which was normal; she was the intruder. Dan was really friendly and an avid collector of vinyl records. He had hundreds and hundreds, mostly rock guitars. There was music playing in the flat from morning till night, with Dan accompanying the records on his guitar. They got along well, all things considered.

However, there was a true lack of privacy. It wasn't only that; Lili's relationship with Jay was changing, not really for the better. Jay worked late more often than not during the week, or he was tired after rugby training. The weekends weren't much better because he played in matches. Jay received many letters from the older woman, the wife of his friend in Philadelphia, and some phone calls late at night. Those letters and calls seriously irked Lili, and she would often start rows about them. She gave Jay an ultimatum, either the correspondence and the phone calls stopped, or their relationship would end. They did stop, for a while.

Life was going to be easier for Lili when she had her driving licence. She was learning to drive, courtesy of Jay's parents as a birthday present. The idea was to share Jay's car until she found one to buy in her price range. She could go to Jay's rugby matches in the London suburbs and also drive to visit the theatres for work without having to spend endless hours on public transport.

Sean, her driving instructor, was Irish. He was forever telling her stories about his family in Belfast and would make her hoot with laughter. He always had a good joke to tell, like the one about Paddy. Paddy went into a shoe shop to buy some wellington boots, wellies as the Irish call them. He asked for his shoe size 10. When the shop assistant brought a pair for him to try on, they fitted perfectly. He paid and went home. However, he came back the following week carrying the wellies. The shop assistant was puzzled and asked if there was a problem, to which he replied there was a small one. He wanted to know if she could lengthen the string that tied the boots together so he could walk faster!

Sean was great; he had complete confidence in Lili's capability to drive, even when she made silly mistakes or when she was over-taking a big lorry on the main road when visibility wasn't good. Unsurprisingly she passed her driving test first time, even during London's rush hour traffic. She said it was all thanks to Sean because he had made her feel at ease and confident behind the wheel.

Lili had enrolled in yoga classes and went twice a week. Meditation was good for her soul, and the exercise helped her sleep better.

Elsa-May phoned Lili one Saturday morning in Hampstead. She was very irate and cross that Lili was 'living in sin' with Jay in London

"What am I going to tell the neighbours about your situation? It's not on, and it's not right that you're living out of wedlock. You're living in sin."

"Well, Mum, if you don't tell the neighbours or anyone else you know up North about my situation, nobody will find out, will they? Anyway, I'm not going to get married just to please your neighbours. Look how your marriage turned out."

Lili was angry but sorry she had spoken so disrespectfully to Elsa-May; they were from different generations. Jay had heard all the commotion and raised voices and said to Lili later that evening, they could get married if it would make things better and easier with her mother. Lili ignored his remarks because she hadn't thought through 'the getting married process' and didn't want anyone to think, least of all herself, that she was getting married just to please her mother's neighbours. The subject was never brought up again.

Some months passed; Dan had gotten into the habit of staying with his girlfriend during the week and was only at their flat with her during weekends. The four of them cooked together and liked to debate different subjects while eating; life was convivial. One evening in the week, after meeting Jay in the local Chinese restaurant for dinner, they were walking home and climbing down the steps to the garden flat when Jay shouted:

"Lili, you left the lights on again. I keep telling you to turn them off when we go out; the electricity bill is high enough as it is. You forgot again when you came to meet me."

Lili was very surprised because she always made a point to check in each room that the lights were off before going out and locking the door.

"Hey, wait a minute; I definitely turned off all the lights. I'm certain. I'd rather spend money on going away for long weekends than giving it to the Electricity Board."

Jay went to unlock the door, but it was already unlocked and slightly ajar. He walked through the hall towards their bedroom and heard some noise from inside. He called out. Then heard some glass shattering. It was a man going headfirst, wearing a leather balaclava, through the window and running off, jumping over the fence. Nothing was missing as far as they could tell, but the convertible bed sofa in the living room had been completely ruined, slashed with knife cuts. Jay phoned the police; they arrived relatively quickly to take a statement and fingerprints and have a look around. That's all they could do.

Three nights later, Lili couldn't sleep. She was still afraid after the incident and wondered whether the intruder would come back again as he was obviously looking for something specific. He must have picked the lock. Suddenly, she heard someone stepping on the broken glass outside. The window had been repaired, but not all the broken glass had been removed. She held her breath and was shaking as she peeked carefully through the curtains and saw a short, slim young man looking through the living room window, wearing what looked like thick black tights and a long-sleeved tight-fitting T-shirt, then he climbed up the small tree in the middle of the garden staring at the house. Lili carefully woke Jay and immediately but discreetly phoned the police, who arrived on the scene within minutes.

The three policemen had arrested the bloke, and he was handcuffed to a lamp post in the street. The police asked Lili and Jay if they could identify him, asking if he was the person they had seen jumping and escaping through the window a few nights ago. Unfortunately, they could not say for sure because it had been dark. They went to the police station to make a statement. Six months later, they heard from the police that they had charged the man as a 'Peeping Tom' and he had appeared in court. He had a long police record as a cat burglar, but Lili and Jay had not seen him steal anything. They just saw him looking into the flat; it was the only charge they could hold against him, the only one that would stick.

The insurance had paid for a new sofa and new door locks. Lili remained perplexed and afraid. Lili and Jay decided to move; living in a garden flat was nice in the summer, but it was an easy target for thieves since it was hidden from street view.

Every morning Lili bought the newspapers, and when she reached the office, she would scan the 'properties to rent' section. She was looking for an unfurnished, rent-controlled flat on the Piccadilly tube line that would take her directly to her office. Flat rental prices in London were horrendous, that's why they wanted a rent-controlled one. They wouldn't have Dan to share the rent when they left. After five months of disappointments and visiting some dreadful properties and buildings, she finally found one in the Evening Standard newspaper that sounded great; it was in West London. She made an appointment for a visit at six o'clock that same day, gave Jay the address and asked him to meet her there.

They were first in line, and they both adored the flat immediately. It was her dream come true; they could leave Hampstead and live together alone, get out of the garden flat where she was always jumpy and scared after the two incidents. It had two bedrooms; the smaller one could be used by Jay as an office, so he wouldn't spend so much time at his work location. And who knows, she thought, it could have another use later on if the stalk flew-by with a little bundle. A story her mother used to tell them when they were kids about how children arrived. It was on the second floor of a detached Victorian house on a quiet road; they could even use the front and back gardens. There was a security code to get into the building. The living room was big with two double bay windows and led off into a small but well-designed kitchen.

Jay was generous and let Lili have carte blanche to decorate how she wanted, and he paid for most of the furniture. She looked in all the house and home magazines and got lots of ideas, finally settling on a warm taupe colour for the paintwork throughout with white and beige wallpaper and a thick eggshell-white fitted carpet throughout. It was cosy and comfortable, and it was their home.

Lili was now at peace and leading an enjoyable professional and social life, she still missed Jen more than she could say, but she also missed something she couldn't fathom. She enjoyed going on holidays abroad with Jay in the winter to The Canaries and in the summer to Scandinavia or Italy, but something was definitely missing, something intangible. They had never used any form of contraception since moving into their new home; Lili could fall pregnant at any time. Perhaps that was what she needed; perhaps that was her missing element.

Chapter Eight
THE MELTDOWN

Things started to change.

Jay bawled at Lili when she started complaining again about the phone calls from Philadelphia late at night and the air mail letters that arrived regularly. On their most recent holiday in Cornwall, Jay had hardly spoken. He was distant, never touching or kissing her. He was always feeling nauseous and anxious, and couldn't sleep. He had consulted a doctor a colleague had recommended. The doctor thought Jay's symptoms were mainly psychosomatic and gave him some mild tranquillisers to take in the evening before going to bed. He had lost his libido, and Lili felt wretched and so unloved.

The health problem apparently stemmed from Jay's conflicts with the HQ in Philadelphia. The Chairman did not agree with how Jay was running the London outfit or with his business plan. Jay decided to negotiate his departure, open his own company, go freelance, get clients and run the business in the beginning from their flat. When he received the money from his grievance package, he went into top gear and became his old self. He had found two potential clients in London, but a very big one based in Philadelphia wanted to sign right away, well, well, well.

Jay was actually in Philadelphia and had been there for over a month. Lili had only spoken to him three times, including the phone call telling her to get out of London and go on a trip.

"Lili, hey Lili, it's me, Anthony; you are daydreaming? I've lost you; you're not focusing. Speak to me, *âllo, âllo!*"

Lili's mind came back to the present time, in Paris, sitting with Anthony in the hotel reception with sister Ivy sleeping in their room upstairs.

"Wow, excuse me, Anthony, I was deep in thought. My mind went way back to years ago, remembering how I met my boyfriend Jay and about our life together. Then all my childhood memories came flooding back with many others. Listen, Anthony, I think the best thing to do is for you to give me your phone number. When I'm back in London next week, I'll call you, and we'll see what, if anything, we can work out."

Anthony kissed her good night the Parisian way- three times on her cheeks; one for the father, one for the son, and one for the holy ghost! He said he would be waiting for her call and wished her a bon voyage.

At 31 years of age, Anthony was enticing, but frankly, she asked herself if she needed that right now. Lili was 24 years young, but she was uncannily street-wise. She realised her relationship with Jay was in shreds.

Ivy was sound asleep when Lili fell into bed in the early hours of the morning - *tomorrow's another day* - she thought and turned off the bedside light and went straight to sleep in the arms of Morpheus, the God of sleep and dreams. *Was it his father, Hypnos, who was playing with her mind tonight?*

The next morning, their last one in Paris, the sisters briskly packed their things after showering, dressing, and putting on their 'faces'. They left their small suitcases at the hotel reception to pick up before getting the airport bus from the station at Les Invalides, which was within walking distance of the hotel. Their flight back to London Heathrow was at five o'clock. They still had time to do some tourist things. It was early Sunday morning, and the sun was already hot. Walking out into the street, they were amazed to see it had been turned into a street market. That explained all the hullabaloo and noise since five o'clock. The receptionist told them that type of food market was typical in most districts of Paris on Sunday morning. Afterwards, everything would close, and shops and markets would not reopen until Tuesday morning.

They sat on the terrace of the Boulangerie next door and ordered two *cafés au lait* and croissants. They were not terribly hungry but were fascinated by all the hullabaloo. There were people everywhere, and the food stands were so beautifully displayed and stacked. Customers gesticulated with their hand language. Lili thought that if their hands were tied behind their backs or cut off, they wouldn't be able to communicate; it looked so funny, so French. Later they took photos of the brightly coloured Mediterranean fish, local fruits and vegetables. They admitted never having seen produce like that back in England.

"I can see you're in a bit of a turmoil this morning, Luv; do you want to talk about it?"

"Sorry, Ivy, I didn't realise it was quite so obvious, but yes, this trip has opened my eyes to a lot of things going on in my life back in London that could and should be better. I can't explain it, but I just know that Paris is the place where I should move to and settle, at least for a while. We've had such good times here together on this short trip, and we've seen many splendid monuments, but there is still so much I want to see and do here. I think I'll come back next weekend, Anthony invited me, and I'm actually already looking forward to it."

"Blimey, hells bells Lili, you're really decisive, and I can see your mind is made up. What if you fall in love with Anthony, and you've only just met him? What will you say to Jay? What will you do?"

"Really, I don't know yet; let's see what happens and cross one bridge at a time. I don't think Jay's got me on his mind. He's busy working, and I would bet my bottom-dollar he's having an affair with that older woman in Philadelphia. Let's enjoy the next few hours of our time in Paris and think about the next step when we get back to England."

The sisters walked to the Grand Palais on the Avenue Winston-Churchill that was built for the fifth '*Exposition Universelle*' of 1900, inaugurated on the 14th of April, 1900, during the Third French Republic, by President Emile Loubet.

Besides the permanent expositions at the Grand Palais that day, there was a temporary one of Impressionist art by the painters Monet, Turner and Whistler that would last for another three weeks. Lili would definitely have liked to see it, but they didn't have enough time.

Lili adored the three French, English and American artists, but her preferred one was the Englishman Joseph Mallord William Turner. She had seen his paintings in the National Gallery in London. The one she particularly liked, her favourite, was the 'Fighting Temeraire'. The ghostlike colours against a triangle of blue sky and rising mist make the scene seem so unreal, like a vision in a dream. The painting depicts the HMS Temeraire being towed by a paddle steam boat on its last journey before it was destroyed and used for scrap. It had played a role in the Battle of Trafalgar, won in 1805 by Lord Nelson against the Franco-Spanish Armada. Lili thought it only right and proper that the painting hung in the National Gallery in Trafalgar Square. It was on loan right now from England to Le Grand Palais, Paris.

Later, while flying back over the English Channel, the sisters were enjoying a gin 'n' tonic, toasting the unforgettable weekend they had spent together and hopefully to many more.

Returning to the office on Monday morning was hard. Ivy was still with Lili because she was on her way to Euston Station to get the Inter-City train back to Chester. She was anxious to start looking for a job. Lili jokingly said to Ivy that someone should hire her quickly while she was a teenager and still knew everything… ha-ha!

During coffee at their desks after Ivy took the train, Lili told Igor and Betty about their wonderful Parisian adventures; they listened fervently. Igor was very familiar with France, spoke the language fluently and was a great connoisseur of French wines and French history.

Lili waited until Tuesday evening to phone Anthony. She still had no news from Jay. Anthony was enthusiastic about wanting to see her again the forthcoming weekend in Paris. Lili was nervous, trying to make excuses not to go. She told him again she was in a relationship, but there was nobody deafer than those who didn't want to hear.

Lili left the office at Friday lunchtime. The business was very quiet; it was the silly summer season. She said she wasn't feeling well and had a migraine coming on. Betty told her to go. Igor had ordered some films from the Distributors that he had missed seeing during the previous weeks to watch in their own private cinema in the basement of their building, as usual on Friday afternoons. He didn't need Lili for that. She didn't want to tell anyone except Ivy that she was returning to Paris. No need for any chins to wag or for anyone to worry. She headed straight out to Heathrow airport for her 3:05 pm British Airways flight to Paris-Orly. Anthony was going to meet her at the flight exit. He always finished work at 4.00 pm on Fridays, and with the one-hour time difference between France and England, it was perfect timing.

Driving into Paris from the airport sitting close to Anthony in his small Lotus Elan car, pleased Lili no end. She was into the spirit of the weekend and wanted to have fun and be frivolous. Anthony handled the car well, full of self-confidence. He winked when he said there was no space in the back for a mother-in-law.

They went to Anthony's big studio to drop off her bag in the rue Lecourbe in the fifteenth district that over-looked a small square with high trees and big bushes in full bloom. Lili washed and changed into a white cotton mini skirt and a fuscia-coloured top, and white canvas shoes. It was a humid summer evening and still hot outside; she was excited and ready to go. Anthony looked relaxed and behaved like a gentleman. There was only one big double bed in the studio, no sofa.

"Oh well," she said to herself, "we'll see later."

Discovering that area in the fifteenth district well away from the usual tourist spots, walking next to Anthony, who had a long stride that she had trouble keeping up with, seemed the best way to begin her weekend.

"I'm going to take you to a place to eat that's about a twenty-minute walk from my studio called "Salomé". It's really cheap, but that's not why I'm taking you. I'm taking you because it's friendly. You can stop believing, like most people, that all Parisians are rude and impolite. They are different from all others, but you'll get to like them one day. There's no choice of the menu; it's a set three-course meal. Wine, sodas and beers are extra. The food is delicious and homemade by Salomé herself, a middle-aged Jewish lady who lives alone but likes to have company; open from Monday to Friday. There's only one service at 8.00 pm, first come, first served. She closes around 10.00 pm. There's no waitress service, so we must go to the counter, help ourselves and pay in cash. You're my guest."

On arrival, there was a small queue. Stepping down into the restaurant, which was in a basement decorated in bright colours with posters of Paris on the walls, Lili saw there were three long wooden tables for twelve people with benches to sit-on at either side. Most of the customers knew each other; they were obviously regulars. Salomé remembered everyone's name and had something pleasant to say to each of them. Anthony told Lili he went to Salomé's twice a week because it felt like home. Lili loved the food; they spent the next two hours talking to some other customers sitting at their long table. Lili was surprised that nearly everyone spoke English, she was embarrassed not to be able to speak a word of French, but it didn't seem to matter.

After the wholesome meal, they walked to the corner of Rue de la Convention and rue de Vaugirard, the latter being 4.3 kilometres long, the longest street in the city. Anthony explained that when you look on a map, Paris districts are shaped like a snail and start with the first district in the centre of Paris at Les Halles, which is a historical centre dating back to the Middle Ages.

"Just for the record," he said, "the smallest street in Paris is Rue des Dégres in the second arrondissement – second district - which is only 5.75 metres long."

They sat and drank coffee for a while and watched people walk by. One of the Parisians' favourite hobbies is 'people watching'.

"Anthony, where are you from in France? Do you have a family?

"I'm from the Alps, one of the eight mountain regions in Metropolitan France, close to the Swiss border. My father owns a sports shop and sells everything for skiing and hiking. My mother owns a library and stationery shop. I go to see them nearly every other weekend in the winter to ski, leaving work at four o'clock. I get to their place late evening on Fridays and am already on the slopes at nine o'clock on Saturdays before the crowds arrive."

"If you like, we could go there, and I could teach you to ski. My eldest brother lives in a town close to our parents with his wife and daughters. My youngest brother lives with his wife and children three metro stops from where I live. I'll take you to meet them tomorrow night if you like. My mother despairs I will never get married and worries I will become an old bachelor."

Lili spent the night in Anthony's arms, talking and stroking each other, they were both relaxed, and it felt good to be connected like that. Anthony made no move to have sex, and Lili was pleased because she wanted and needed time to think about how her life and attitude were starting to change. As the dawn came up and the light was entering through the large open window, they fell asleep side by side like carefree children.

Jonathan was the name of Anthony's youngest brother. They arrived at his flat at seven o'clock on Saturday with a small bouquet of violets and a bottle of Saint Emilion wine from the Bordeaux region. They were exhausted after the day's walking, getting on and off metros and buses, and visiting Les Invalides with a professional guide, which she and Ivy had not had time to do. They also visited Le Grand Palais for the Impressionist exposition. Lili loved it and was happy to see the Monet, Turner and Whistler paintings.

Anthony said he enjoyed seeing it, too, despite his lack of interest in the arts because he preferred sports to art.

Lili was embarrassed arriving at the brother's flat and didn't know how to explain her presence in Paris, but Jonathan didn't ask any questions, and neither did his lovely wife, Claire. They made her feel very welcome, chatted in good English and served entrecôte steaks, French fries, cheese and a Tarte-Tatin – upside-down apple pie, especially for Lili. Claire loved Scotland and had travelled there three times. She said she had a thing about men in kilts, and Jonathan thought it hysterical.

Sunday passed too quickly, and she found herself at Orly airport in the early evening, practically in tears, when Anthony kissed her *au revoi*r lightly on her lips.

"Lili, *au revoir* does not mean goodbye; it means to see you again. I really liked being in your company, and I like you more than you can ever imagine. I'm going to think about you all week, and I'll wait for your phone calls. When I drive to work tomorrow with Paul, I know he will ask me about you and everything we did, and I will enjoy telling him and talking about you. Your ears will be burning. I bet he will also ask about Ivy, but as you said, Ivy is too young for him; he'll get over her and soon find another girl to flirt with."

Lili called Anthony several times and stayed on the phone for longer than she should have; it was going to cost a small fortune. At the weekend she received some postcards from him with pictures of Paris, places they had visited together and a short letter. She had been foolish to give him her address, but she was happy she did.

A couple of weeks went by like that; Jay was due to return to London around the second week in October. They had spoken a couple of times over the phone, but they didn't have much to say to each other, just small talk about work and their families.

Lili flew to Paris once again and spent what she thought was going to be her last weekend with Anthony; then, she would go back to her 'normal' life.

"It doesn't have to be the last weekend or the last time we see each other, Lili. Instead, it could be the start of a whole new life together here in France. It seems impossible for me to believe that you would accept to leave London because you have a great job, a boyfriend, a flat, friends and your family not too far away. But think about it. If you are here again with me, it's because things are not good in your life, and if that's true, you have to change. Remember the Stéphane Hessel essay I gave you? We talked about that, if things are not good, change them. I'm serious. I want you to come to live with me. I'll get a bigger flat for us that you can decorate. You can go to school to learn French and afterwards get a job. I have money saved up, and I also earn a good salary for both of us. I could teach you to ski; we could go to many interesting places together. My brother has already told my mother about you, but I don't think she realises how serious I am."

Lili's head was spinning. It was true she was happy being in Anthony's company. They hadn't made love, but something close to it. He was shy in bed but very loving and tender, and she liked the way he kissed her, soft, sweet and long. She couldn't see her life again with Jay; in her mind, she had already moved on.

"Listen, Anthony, it sounds great and very tempting, and I know you are sincere and honest. I'll let you know and give you my answer shortly. I'll talk it through with Mum, Ivy and cousin Jen."

After work and during the weekends, Lili made lots of enquiries on where foreigners could go to learn French in Paris, courses for people who were complete beginners. Incredibly, and after much researching, she found two establishments. One was the Alliance Française on boulevard Raspail, which specialised in teaching French as a foreign language to adult foreigners. The other was the

Sorbonne open university not far from the Latin Quarter. She calculated the costs and did the math. If she took out nearly every penny of her savings, she could afford to do it.

Before her courage failed her, Lili completed the application forms and enrolled at the Alliance Française from the 3rd of January to the 31st of March for two hours in the mornings from Monday to Friday. She was also going to need time to settle-in, get her papers in order and find her way around. She would need to learn to speak French quickly if she wanted to find a job in Paris.

For that reason, she also enrolled at the Sorbonne open university from the 1st of April to the 31st of July full-time, five hours a day, five days a week. In their brochure, they described it as a program to give foreign students, whatever their level, the opportunity to attend French language and culture courses in Paris. There would be an exam and a certificate at the end of the programme. Over the phone she told Anthony.

"Anthony, I've done it. I'm enrolled at both the Alliance Française and the Sorbonne open university; the courses begin on the 3rd of January to the 31st of July. I've paid with my savings, and I'll be able to live for a while on my holiday pay after I leave my job."

"Lili, *ma chérie*, that's the best news I've ever had. I can't believe you are giving up everything to come to live here in Paris with me. You are *redoutable et formidable*"

Two days before Jay was due back home, Lili handed in her resignation to Rob, her boss. She would leave in two months' time on the 10th of December. When she told Igor, he was gob-smacked.

"Lili, *vous êtes folle* - you're crazy, you don't speak a word of French, you don't have a job, who do you know in Paris? You have a great job here; many people envy you, and you also have a great life style. What are you going to say to Jay? You've been together for five years, does he know? Have you told your family? *Mon Dieu,* Lili, think it through again; we can always tear up your resignation letter. Are you really serious? You can't do it, for heaven's sake. Go home and think about it for a day or two. We'll talk about it again on Monday."

Jay was in a taxi on his way to the flat from Heathrow airport; he had phoned Lili as soon as he passed through Customs. She was waiting for him. Lili had already told her mother, Elsa-May, that she would leave London on the 10th of December and spend a couple of weeks, including Christmas, with her and the family in Chester before flying to Paris and starting her new life on the 28th of December.

Elsa-May was sad that Lili was going to live so far away and worried about how she would manage once she got to Paris; they would talk about that over the Christmas period.

Autumn leaves covered the garden that early Saturday morning as Lili was looking at Jay through the window while paying the taxi driver and putting his bags on the pavement in front of the gate. He looked up at her with a half-smile and waved. He looked tired after the long journey and probably hadn't slept much on the overnight flight. Lili still loved Jay; she was still attracted to him; who wouldn't be? But she was no longer in love, not any more. She had matured and moved on in her mind. Jay gave her a hug, and a friendly kiss, not the typed she expected after the long separation.

"Hey Lili, you've lost weight, you're looking a bit skinny, I can feel your bones. How are you? How have things been?"

"Thanks for the compliments! You're looking a bit rough yourself. I'm all right, I suppose; it's been very strange around here during your prolonged absence. Was your trip a success?"

"Oh, yeah, I'm right on schedule with the timing for the computer programmes I wrote and have installed them on their new equipment. They've already paid me for two-thirds of the contract. After the final testing by their team during the next two weeks, the last payment will be sent via a bank transfer. Let's go out tonight, Lili, and celebrate. Right now, I need to get some kip and be out of the door in two hours to watch and cheer on the rugby team playing in an away game in Watford. Obviously, I've not been able to train while I've been away in the States, so they didn't put me on today's team. I phoned Eddy, the Captain, and told him I was back today. I'll start training again on Tuesday and Thursday evenings and see how it goes."

"You've got to be joking; you're off to watch rugby today, your first day back home after months away? We have loads to talk about and catch up on. I can't believe it. I've been waiting for you."

"Give me a break, Lili; I'm tired. You could book a table at Luigi's for nine o'clock. I'll definitely be back by then."

After his power sleep, a wash and a change of clothes, Jay was in his car on the way to Watford for the match. He didn't even ask Lili if she wanted to go; he could see she was as mad as hell, and he wanted to avoid any conflicts today.

Lili could hear her good friend and neighbour, Pauline, walking about upstairs. She went up and knocked on her door. Her little shepherd dog started to bark, and when the door opened, he jumped into her arms; Lili often had him stay when his masters went away for weekends or trips.

"Well, how's that for a welcome! Hi, Pauline, are you free? Is this a good time for us to have a chat and a coffee together?"

"Yes, absolutely, come in. I was just tidying the place after Reg, the whirlwind, left to play football. You and I are both sports widows. I don't know how or why we put up with them. You're not looking too good, what's the matter? Let's go and put the kettle on."

"I've decided to leave Jay. I'll be moving out in December to stay with my family for a couple of weeks in Chester, and then I'm heading off to Paris."

"What, Paris? Now, that is a piece of news. I had seen postcards and letters arriving from France addressed to you. You know how the postman often puts the mail in the wrong boxes. Good job there are only three flats here. Otherwise, we'd never get our post. What brought on the decision? Who is he?"

"I've been feeling lonely for longer than I can remember. Jay is always so distant and absent. We practically never do anything together anymore, and when we do, he's not his old self. He's changed, but we get on together, and I do care about him."

"That's not enough, Lili; just getting on well together in not enough. You get on well with most people. The relationship between a couple should be much deeper and mean much more than just getting on."

"I have decided to spill the beans and tell Jay tonight during dinner at Luigi's or perhaps tomorrow. He's already gone off to support his team. Can you imagine?"

The friends spent the whole afternoon together talking; Pauline helped Lili put her thoughts into perspective. They made a date to go out together during the week after work. Pauline worked for one of the big English banks in the City near Saint Paul's Cathedral. Pauline hugged Lili and told her how much she was going to miss her and gave her friend her unconditional support and told Lili she could always count on her and Reg if she needed a shoulder to cry on, a helping hand, some company or prepare the bags and suitcases for the departure. Lili climbed down the stairs to her flat and took a long soak in the bath with natural oils to relax, then got ready for dinner at Luigi's. It was true she had lost weight, but it suited her.

Jay didn't get back at nine o'clock or ten o'clock. Lili was in bed fast asleep at midnight when he stumbled into the room and slept fully clothed on top of the duvet, drunk as a skunk.

The next morning was very sunny. At ten o'clock, Lili was already dressed in jeans and a V-necked cashmere sweater lounging on the sofa reading, drinking tea, and eating a toasted bacon buttie with brown sauce, similar to the ones her Mum usually made at home on Sunday mornings. Nothing Lili made ever tasted as good as Elsa-May's cooking, no matter how hard she tried. Jay walked into the room, covering his eyes from the sunlight.

"Sorry about last night, Lili, really sorry, I wanted to phone you, but we got carried away in the pub after our incredible win over the Watford team with a score of 27 vs 18. I like the States, but they don't play or watch rugby much. It's hard for us Brits over there; I was truly missing the game."

"No need to apologise; that's par for the course and typical of you. As it's Sunday morning, I vote we drive over to the pub in Kew gardens when you've had a cuppa and a shower, buy the newspapers and have a drink of the hair of the dog that bit you. Sitting at the tables outside will be nice as it's a lovely autumn day. I already fancy a steak and kidney pie with salad and some wine. It will be good to get out today because tomorrow I'll be on the tube and at work the whole day, then I'm scheduled to go with Igor in the evening to our theatre in Maidstone for an event."

Jay was relaxed and talking nonchalantly, sitting with Lili at the big wooden table outside the pub, reading the papers and the Sunday Times magazine, drinking a Guinness and eating a Ploughman's lunch of cheese and bread, like old times. There weren't many customers, and it was quiet. Lili had the jitters, and the palms of her hands were sweating. She had to get it over with and spit out what she had to say.

"There's no easy way to say it, Jay. No use waltzing around; my name's not Matilda. I'm leaving London to live in Paris. I've enrolled in two establishments to learn French and the French Civilisation. I'll begin on the 3rd of January, but before that, on the 10th of December, I'm going to move out of the flat, after I've worked my notice, and stay with Mum in Chester and spend Christmas with the whole family."

"What! Thanks, that's a great homecoming announcement. I'm shuck-up but not really surprised. We've been out of sync for a while. Neither of us is really happy, and I know I make you unhappy. I also realise I'm absent most of the time and not very accessible when I'm here. But don't you think it's a bit drastic, even dramatic, going off to live in another country? Wouldn't it be better if we tried to work it out, tried talking, tried to make another go of things together? What are they going to say at work? Have you thought everything through?"

"Yes, of course, I've thought everything through; I had enough time during your absence. You've been away for months."

You know, Jay, people don't change, they can't change, people get better, or they get worse, but they don't fundamentally change. If I stay, you'll make an effort for a while, and so will I. We'll pretend, and then we'll go back to our old ways. Moving to Paris is what I want to do. While I was there with Ivy, I had the gut feeling, and I know without a shadow of a doubt that Paris is where I ought to live and start a new life. I'm not saying it will be easy, but if I don't try, I'll never know. 'The only things one never regrets are one's mistakes,' as Oscar Wilde said."

"I've told Rob and Igor at work. They tried to dissuade me when I handed in my resignation, but my decision has been made, and I'll reconfirm tomorrow. Even if you had fallen into my arms and told me how much you had missed me when you got back yesterday instead of going out with your rugby mates, I don't think I would have changed my mind. The dice have been thrown; the snowball is rolling."

"Lili, the million-dollar question is, did you meet someone in Paris?"

"Yes, I met someone, but that's not why I'm going. He's not a lover. I'm going because I'm unhappy in my present life with you. I won't pretend that I don't love you, and we can get along well most of the time, but it's not enough. Something, an element, is terribly missing."

"In that case, I can tell you that I did have an affair with 'you know who' while in Philadelphia; I'd never have told you otherwise."

"You bastard, you dirty pig, you big turd, that's the worst thing you could ever have done or said to me. You have punched below the belt. In the five years we've been an equation, I've always dreaded finding out that you slept with that Jane. It's the thing that's always made me feel unhappy and miserable. Anyway, my female instinct already told me. All men are cowards, and you didn't want to phone me often in case your voice or my questioning gave your game away. The difference between you and me is that I haven't had sex with a friend I've met. We may just stay friends. One thing is for sure, even if you got down on your bended knees, I would never have sex with you again. I'll never be able to get the picture out of my head of you and her together. You can put your dick wherever you want now, bugger off, get lost, screw you, drop dead; you're a waste of space, you fuckin' prick."

"Lili, I'm sorry, so sorry. I really didn't mean to hurt you; please, let's try to get through the next few weeks somehow."

"Yeah, all right, let's do that; let's just try to be civil to each other. We'll work something out until I go."

That was that. Lili somehow got through the days; there was an endless list of things to do and organise. Surprisingly, Jay was a real help, never nasty or bitter. He went to stay with his parents for a few days up North to give Lili more privacy in the flat. He told Lili his parents were really sorry about them splitting up, and they hoped Lili was doing the right thing. Jay cooked and talked a lot and was good company when he was there, just like in the old times.

In the meantime, Lili often phoned Anthony and wrote about her feelings and some of her anxieties. She was getting cold feet as the time drew nearer to leave. Anthony banished her fears and told her he had found a one-bedroom flat with a big living room, kitchen and bathroom with a large balcony not far from where he was already living in the same district. They needed to buy furniture, but he wanted to do all those things with Lili.

Anthony was excited but somewhat apprehensive. He had never lived with a girl or woman before. His friend Paul was being very supportive, positive and encouraging as well as his family. He told Lili:

"When I phoned my mother to let her know what we are doing, she nearly had a fatal heart attack. She didn't believe me. She phoned me back the next day after speaking to my youngest brother Jonathan and then Claire. Jonathan confirmed you are a charming, pretty and clever young woman, even if you are from England. They said it's not your fault that the English burned Joan of Arc to death in 1431 during the hundred years war, and they won't hold you personally responsible... ha-ha."

Lili chuckled; she was getting to know and like Anthony's sense of humour.

On her last day in London, Lili's boss and a very good friend, Igor, had organised a leaving party for her with friends from the film industry, Distributors from MGM, Walt Disney, Columbia, Warner Bros and some small private ones from Wardour Street, her colleagues and theatre managers. A big room was hired upstairs in a restaurant on Old Crompton Road. There was standing room only, drinks from the open bar were flowing, and food was in abundance. Everyone was having a good time, as always. Around midnight, before guests started to leave, Igor gave a short speech, very tongue in cheek. He had such a wonderfully dry sense of humour. Nobody delivered a speech better than Igor; he was often invited to make after-dinner speeches. At the end, he wished her good luck *bon voyage* and hoped there would be an "*entente cordiale*" between her and the French, but if not, she could always come back and get her old job or a similar one! Lili was laughing and crying at the same time. She was going to miss Igor and the 'Street'. Igor and his gorgeous wife, Olivia, who was also one of her best friends and lived close by, drove her back to the flat where she slept for the last time. Igor was singing, "*What will I do when you are far away, and I am blue, what will I do?*"

Getting up on that last Saturday morning required a sub-human effort on Lili's part. She wanted to stay under the duvet, hide and not think about anything. She was happy and excited to be going to live in Paris and embraced the thought of her new life abroad. However, leaving Jay and their life together after five years was one of the hardest things she had ever done in her life. Jay was quiet, moving about like a robot, hardly saying a word. He helped Lili get her bags and suitcase down the stairs into the parked car where Pauline and Reg were waiting to say goodbye. With tears in her eyes, Pauline couldn't contain her sadness. Lili swore she would keep in touch and send her the new address in Paris.

Driving along London's Westway towards Euston station for her inter-city train to Chester, Jay put on The Beatles 'Let It Be', which they both liked. They listened and remained silent, both in their own thoughts. Sad. Jay would play rugby in the afternoon; he would be all right. He'd run and get it all out of his system and probably have a good fight or two with the opposing team.

Standing on the platform a few minutes before the train was due to leave, Lili had tears falling down her cheeks in spite of herself.

"Don't cry because it's over; smile because it happened, Lili. I'll always love you. You can't take that away from me. We had our ups and downs, but for me, it was mostly good, with more ups than downs. I realise now, looking back, that I wasn't always there for you, and I left you alone too much, wrapped up in my own world. Sometimes, there wasn't much space for you. I was totally unfair about my relationship with Jane in Philadelphia. I must say, when you told me you were going to leave; I didn't believe you were serious. You had a great job and some great friends; not many people can say they achieved what you did working your way up in the film industry, and a young Lass from Liverpool at that. I asked myself time and time again why would you leave all that behind. I realise what I'm losing, and I also realise you deserve better. I love you universally. You've got gumption and courage; you'll be fine in France with a whole new culture and language to learn. I'll phone you during the week to see how things are going in Chester. Say hello to everyone. Christmas this year is going to be very odd, to say the least, without you at my folks' house."

They kissed and held each other close for the last time.

The train picked up speed on its way to Chester as the light snowfall became a blizzard.

Elsa-May and Lili stuck together like superglue during the two weeks leading up to Lili's departure to Paris. Elsa-May didn't want Lili to go to Paris, and neither did anyone. They avoided the subject as if walking on eggs. They shopped until they dropped, literally, for presents, decorations, food and drinks for Christmas. The house was going to be full of guests on the 24th, 25th, and Boxing Day on the 26th, including cousin Jen with Pete, Dotty, Jen's mother, who was also Elsa-May's sister, Lili's eldest brother Lee and a girlfriend, Lili's youngest brother Rod and a girlfriend from university, and last but not least, Ivy. There were plenty of rooms in the three-storey house, but they were going to be short of beds. Elsa-May ordered some mattresses, which she had put on the floor in the two living rooms at bedtime for her two sons and their girlfriends.

Ivy and Lili wrapped many presents, wrote lots of Christmas cards for Elsa-May and themselves and decorated the tree and put-up fairy lights around all the windows and some doors. They even built a snowman in the back garden with the usual carrot for a nose and a woolen hat and were exhausted removing all the snow from the pavement, but it was such fun. Lili loved spending time with Ivy; the activities kept her mind totally occupied. They talked a lot together about her move to Paris. Lili was starting to relax and looked forward to the festivities and drinking champagne.

Jay phoned as promised; they were like strangers. He spoke about finances. Jay had decided to transfer money each month into the account that Lili was going to open when she arrived in Paris. It was to reimburse her for all the items in the flat she had bought over the years and had left behind, plus some 'run away money' as he called it. He said he was doing fine, but Lili knew he would never admit his true feelings. He was going up North himself for a week or two to spend Christmas and New Year with his parents, brother and nephews. There were no rugby matches or training planned until the New Year because of the snow and because half of the team was on holiday.

Despite everything, Jay wanted them to stay in touch; he was worried about Lili, though he said he wasn't. She was a very determined person, even pig-headed at times, and he wanted to know that she was all right and safe.

Anthony phoned Lili every day, sometimes twice a day, as if he had doubts that she would get on the aeroplane on the 28th of December. He reassured her that Paul agreed to loan him his car, the big Peugeot 504, to bring her and the luggage to the new flat, their new flat. He was going to the Alps for a week to celebrate Christmas and to ski with his eldest brother and some friends. Moreover, he intended to tell everyone about Lili. Surprise, surprise.

Chapter Nine

LIVING ON THE CONTINENT

"I love these times, just the two of us sitting here in front of the open log fire drinking hot chocolate before going to bed. Oh, Mum, it's been the best Christmas ever. I loved the way we did the old traditional things like putting up the Christmas stockings over the mantelpiece, and everyone opening presents together while drinking sherry and port before dinner and smelling the stuffed turkey and trimmings cooking in the oven. I don't care what anyone says; Christmas is not Christmas without a stuffed turkey. Your home-made Christmas pudding nearly got us all drunk with the amount of brandy you poured in it. Great family recipe; you must give it to me for next year. I don't know where I'll be."

Lili stopped in her tracks by her own words.

"Lili, try your best to come back as often as you can, especially at Christmas. I love us to be together at this time of year. Everyone does his own thing throughout the year, but Christmas is a family occasion. I hope and pray you'll be all right in France. You don't know that man Anthony very well and have no guarantee what so ever it will work out between you. It's not a good thing going from one man to another without an interim break. It seems to me you're on the rebound. I know I gave you a hard time when I learned you were living with Jay in London, and I wanted you to get married. This new situation is different; don't jump in with both feet. Wait and see; give yourselves time to get to know each other well."

"You're just a natural worrier, Mum, like all mums. If you didn't worry, you wouldn't be a mum. Anyway, you know how the saying goes: a son is a son until he is wed, and a daughter is a daughter until she is dead. I'll be back, and Paris is only an hour's direct flight from Liverpool. It's not like I'm going to Australia like cousin Stan. By the way, I'm not on the rebound, my relationship with Anthony hasn't really started, and we're not lovers. I'll phone and write to you as much as possible. I'll be busy trying to learn French and seeing about getting a job. I hope I'll make some friends quickly. Anyway, Jonathan and Claire, Anthony's brother and sister-in-law, are really nice; you'd like them, they live a few metro stations away, and I'm looking forward to getting to know them better as well as their three little kids, just as soon as I can speak the lingo. Let's go to bed now, call it a day and get some sleep. Lee will be driving me to the airport tomorrow afternoon. He's such a good older brother and great support; I've still got a million and one things to do in the morning before getting into that car."

What am I doing? Lili was thinking to herself, sitting alone in a window seat on the Air France flight to Paris-Orly on the 28th of December- the fateful day. She was thinking about the hugs with Elsa-May, Ivy, and Rod before getting into Lee's old Volkswagen car to the airport. Christmas had been wonderful. They set-off early because it had started snowing again, and they didn't want any delays on the motorway. On the journey, Lee told her not to be too proud, and if it didn't work out in Paris, she should get on a flight back to England and go home to Mum. He was a brick, always playing the role of the big protective brother with good pieces of sound advice. Lee stayed until Lili had checked-in her baggage, they hugged, then he turned and walked away, he hated good-byes as much as she did.

As Lili was getting off the flight, amongst other things, she was wondering what arrangements, if any, Anthony had made to celebrate New Year's Eve in three days' time.

She saw him standing at the end of the moving stairs, looking tall and very French in a full-length grey pigskin leather coat and roll-neck jumper. He was tanned from his trip to the Alps and looked so handsome but shy and vulnerable; her heart melted. She could tell he was also feeling nervous as soon as he spotted her. Lili had tried to look her best. Her hair was swinging, and her make-up, different shades of blue eye shadows to match her big blue eyes, looked good. Her black high heel boots made her look taller, and she was slimmer despite all the food she had eaten over the holidays. *That would be my new resolution*, she thought, *put an end to gluttony*.

Jokingly, acting like a movie star, Anthony gave her a full welcome kiss and took her gloved hand in his. They looked into each other's eyes and smiled. It was going to be all right.

The weather was mild, totally different from England's. This was the Continent! Lili opened the door to the second-floor flat, the second floor, just like in London, and walked in towards the double French windows leading onto the balcony. It was chic; she loved the wooden parquet floors. There were only a few sticks of furniture in the living room, the bare essentials, a coffee table, and two stools. Anthony had bought a huge bed that was in the centre of the bedroom. He looked embarrassed and said that's all he had time to buy because his rented studio was furnished. Luckily there were big fitted cupboards in the hall and bedroom with plenty of hanging space and lots of drawers.

"Don't worry, Lili, after dinner tonight at Salomé's and a good night's sleep in our new big bed; we'll go out tomorrow and buy everything we need. The sales have already started in some shops since Christmas is over. The important thing is that we are together."

Lili was happy lying beside Anthony naked in their new bed. They had drunk some wine at Salomé's and were both feeling relaxed. They had no lamps yet and were in the dark. The only light was coming from outside through the closed shutters. They were discovering each other slowly. Other than a few flirts, Lili had only known one man, Jay, and he had been the love of her life. This situation was new and exciting. She was enjoying Anthony's attention, but he never made a move to possess her sexually. He told her not to be afraid. He wanted her to make the moves; he would not resist her, but he was unable to be the initiator.

Lili understood and did everything she knew to arouse him, and it worked; he entered her, and it was a release for them both. All tensions and strain were seeping away and becoming glorious; they both felt and experienced the climax at the same moment. Afterwards, in each other's arms, Anthony said it would always be that way; if she wanted him, she should come to him. Lili had a healthy libido, and she sensed they would be more than fine together.

Lili felt tenderness towards Anthony. He seemed defenceless; she wanted to protect him, like a mother. *Was that it?* She thought, *is this relationship going to work because I'm developing maternal instincts, and he wants or needs a mother? Wait and see.* They fell into a deep sleep and woke late the next day hungry and thirsty. They quickly showered, dressed and hurried to the nearest café for some breakfast. Anthony smoked French cigarettes while drinking his black coffee. Lili loved tea, any tea, especially Earl Grey. She drank a pot at each breakfast. She usually ate cereal, but now she was eating croissants and baguettes; she thought it was very decadent.

"Anthony, we must buy some things for the kitchen like dishes, crockery, pans, a frying pan, a kettle, some cutlery and of course a teapot for me and a coffee pot for you. Luckily the kitchen is equipped with a stove, fridge and best of all a dishwasher. I don't mind cleaning or ironing, but I hate washing dishes. Oh, and we simply must buy some food and drinks. We can't eat our meals out every day."

Her practicality caused Anthony to laugh. He called her 'Darling' for the first time, and after that, he always called and referred to her as Darling.

"Let's make a list of the essentials; then we'll go to Galleries Lafayette in Montparnasse, which is the nearest big store that sells everything. It will be sensible to set a budget; otherwise, we'll have to hold-up a bank if my savings can't buy everything. I'll phone Paul to see if he wants to give us a hand. If he does, we can use his big Peugeot to bring things home if the Galleries don't deliver on the same day."

Paul met them in the shop an hour later. Anthony's personality changed with Paul around. He let him make the decisions- always agreeing with him, was shy and reserved in his company. Lili didn't know what to make of the scene. It was as if she wasn't there; he was unable to see her.

They made headway and bought all the things for the kitchen that they were able to put in the car, as well as the bed linen, bathroom towels and two contemporary-style bedroom lamps. The shop was to deliver the green suede convertible sofa, the bedside tables and the big lamps on the 31st.

"We're so clever and organized – what a trio. We did really well. We can get the curtains, washing machine, iron, etcetera next week. We can take our things to my brother Jonathan's flat to wash and iron in the meantime if need be. He's away at Claire's family home in Normandy for the holiday period but left me their keys. By the way," he said, "*Bienvenu en France* - welcome to France."

Paul invited them to eat at his place in the evening, a two-bedroom flat with, funnily enough, a Scottish look about it, cosy yet sophisticated. His widowed mother, who adored her only child and lived across the street, had done the shopping as per Paul's instructions. It was a simple cold meal but exquisite, and Paul was an attentive host. Anthony was still not himself, not the person she had come to know, but he was relaxing after a large glass of the 12-year-old Glenfiddich whiskey. Around midnight Lili started yawning and wanted to get home. Paul phoned a taxi as they had been drinking. He gave Lili the three Parisian kisses on her cheeks: one for The Father, one for The Son and one for the Holy Ghost, shook Anthony's hand and bid them a good night with a wide grin.

Anthony was quiet when they got back. He said he was tired, too. There was a lot to do, everything they had bought during the day was piled up in the hall and living room, but they went straight to bed and slept like logs.

It was the 30th of December morning, nearly New Year's Eve, Lili's first one away from her close friends and family. Lili had made breakfast in her new home and was trying to store and shelve all the items they had bought the previous day. She was keeping herself busy, trying not to think too much.

"What will we do tomorrow for New Year's Eve? Have you got anything planned? I don't know anyone here except Paul, who told me he was going by train with his mother for a few days to celebrate with some cousins in Britany."

"Oh, sorry, I forgot to tell you, we've been invited to my cousin Flavie's flat near Montparnasse. The few people I know in Paris all live in this area, which is close to the Maine-Montparnasse area. Personally, I think the Tower of Montparnasse is the ugliest building in Paris, all black and oppressive looking. I'm told it's also the tallest at 210 metres with fifty-nine floors. One of the best places, as far as I'm concerned, is inside at the top. Its 360° panorama view is exceptional. At least if you're inside the tower, you can't see its ugly facade! We should go up to the restaurant one afternoon at tea time or have a cocktail at the bar in the evening and see Paris by night all lit up."

"Who's going to be there, what's the dress code and do we need to bring something?"

"You know I love meeting people, going out and dressing up, but I feel really shy about meeting some of your family and friends because I don't know how to speak French yet."

"Don't worry about bringing anything. We will be told how much it costs per head, and I'll write a cheque to Flavie. We should arrive at ten o'clock in the evening wearing an evening dress. I suppose, like all women, you've certainly got a little black dress."

They made a handsome couple when they arrived and were greeted by cousin Flavie and her husband, Adam. They had taken the children to stay with Flavie's mother, who lived on the third floor, two floors up. They were looking forward to eating, dancing and hosting their guests. A big table for twelve was laid in the huge living room. It looked amazing, with crystal glasses, silver cutlery, white gold-rimmed bone china crockery, flowers and decorations. Very posh. Lili was glad she had made an effort with her dress, hair and makeup. Anthony was in a good mood, and Lili was delighted that Flavie spoke fluent English. She had lived in England for a few years as an Au Pair and then as a translator. The other guests who arrived were their hosts' friends from university or colleagues from work.

Everyone was drinking champagne and other aperitifs and bombarding Lili with questions like, what type of university degree do you have? Where do you come from? Do you ski? Why did the English burn Joan of Arc? Lili wanted Anthony to come to her rescue, but he left her to it and sat on one of the other sofas reading comic books. Adam bought and owned hundreds of them and had an amazing collection that would be worth a lot of money in years to come. They started to eat at eleven o'clock. Lili was sitting opposite Anthony and was horrified because the first course was oysters and seafood, which she had never eaten before in her life. The look of it made her stomach churn. She waited for the next course, which was foie gras with hot toast, which she loved.

At midnight they heard the bells chiming; they all kissed in the Parisian style, opened the windows and banged wooden spoons in pans on the balcony, made lots of noise, and blew whistles. In the alleys, cars were honking their horns by the hundreds; generally, people were going crazy and in high spirits. It was such fun. Lili went over to Anthony to wish him a happy New Year; he was shy again in front of everyone and did not return her kiss. She pretended not to notice.

The dinner continued after drinking a Trou Normand - a Normandy hole - which was lime and lemon sorbets served in small glasses with Calvados alcohol, distilled from Normandy apples, poured over the sorbet. Flavie thought it helped digest the first courses and made room in the stomach for the next ones, which were cured hams, stuffed cold meats, and an amazing cheese board. There were at least twelve varieties from different regions all over France, including goat's cheese. They talked all night about food, comparing each dish to another and one region to another. It was simply divine. An argument was going on about how many varieties of cheese France produced. The argument went from 450 to 1500, but they all agreed there were eight categories of cheese grouped into families. Lili was as full-up as she had ever been in her entire life.

At three o'clock, Flavie put on some vinyl records, and everyone began to dance and rock 'n' roll. Lili didn't know how to rock. Pleasantly surprised, Anthony taught Lili the basic steps; he was an agile dancer and knew lots of passes. Light on his feet and in sync with the music, he was not in the least bit tired. Lili was impressed and really enjoyed dancing the rock 'n' roll with him.

They ate a desert of Norwegian omelette flambé au cognac. A basket of fresh fruits was placed on the table. Around five o'clock, digestives were served, Cognac, Armagnac, old whiskeys, Cointreau, and fruit juices with still and sparking water. The guests left the table and started chatting in groups or dancing. It was a superb night; Lili had never imagined she could sit at a table the whole night eating and drinking, especially such fine foods and wines. The cherry on the cake in her mind was she had learned to dance the rock. *This is how the French do things, and in style,* she thought.

Lili was getting tired of listening to the French language, trying to understand and participate in some of the conversations whenever she heard words she recognised. She wondered how she was going to manage. A few more people arrived at seven o'clock in the morning, cousins and neighbours, kissing and offering good wishes. La soupe à l'oignion – onion soup - was served, as the tradition requires, after a long food orgy before the guests began to leave. After so much drinking, most of them took the metro home or stayed and slept on the sofas. Lili and Anthony walked the distance to their flat in half an hour, giving them time to sober up and see Paris begin a new day, a new year. They fell into bed at ten o'clock, after twelve hours of partying, flinging their clothes all over the chairs and joking that they would not be in time to attend the church service.

Lili had lost her faith a number of years ago, probably when moving to London. It had happened slowly but surely. She didn't believe in God but somehow believed in black, not white; this was a contradiction in terms, she knew. She was confused and needed to think deeply about the subject of religion; one day, she would. Anthony said he was not a

Christian, more of an agnostic. He believed in science. He had been brought-up partially by an old maiden aunt who wanted to become a Nun but was prevented from doing so when she agreed to help raise three young boys while her niece and her husband were occupied running their businesses in the Alps. She was frustrated and consequently became extremely strict and unkind.

Anthony and his two brothers had suffered. Anthony, who was the middle son, had been humiliated. He believed that was how he lost his faith. One of the keys to happiness is a bad memory, and he tried never to think about his lost youth.

As in most countries around the world, January 1st was a bank holiday, an official day-off in France; Anthony didn't have to go to work. Lili wanted to phone her mother and sister, but they did not have a phone in their Parisian flat. Anthony had ordered a telephone line to be installed like in his furnished studio, but the wait list was long, very long.

The third President of the Fifth French Republic, Monsieur Valéry Giscard d'Estaing, at 48 years of age, was the youngest French President of France. Upon his election in 1974, the previous year, he had made an election promise that on every street corner in France, a telephone box would be installed within two years and a telephone in every home, upon request, within the year. The French were far behind the Brits in telecommunications; Lili was really frustrated. They went to the street café where telephone booths could be found armed with lots of French franc coins allowing Lili to make a call to Chester. She was so happy to have spoken to everyone. There was a real family buzz, but afterwards, alone with Anthony in the flat, she became melancholic and homesick. *This is only to be expected, don't dwell on it*, she thought.

"I'll have to go to the French administration tomorrow to apply for my carte de séjour - residency permit – because I'll need one to start my French lessons at the Alliance Française in two days' time. I can't believe I'm going back to school; it feels so weird. The United Kingdom entered the European Economic Community (EEC) in January 1973 under the premiership of Edward Heath, all the bureaucratic paperwork between the member nations should be a thing of the past, but I've heard how the French bureaucracy can make a sane man lose his mind and become completely bonkers. That's the price I have to pay to begin a new life in gay Paris, but it's cheap at the price, don't you think?"

"Yeah, you'll become bonkers, ha-ha, great word, but you must already be bonkers to come here and live with me, Mister and Mrs. Bonkers!"

"You know that word. You're so clever; come next to me on the sofa, you smooth-talking froggy. I'm in the mood for love and the first kisses of the new year. If you don't come, I'm going to tickle you to death. Stop being so shy all the time. You can touch me; I'm not going to break or eat you alive."

Once again, it was Lili who made the first move; Anthony let himself be seduced on the sofa, but he was never the seducer. Lili came each time they had sex, she wanted to climax, and she did. She didn't know if she was in love with him, but she liked him and cared for him a lot, which was the next best thing. She was giving herself time, time to fall in love, get settled, and get used to them as a couple. However, she got the impression he was thinking about something or someone else whenever they were naked together, and she was afraid it wasn't just an impression. She forced herself not to think about Jay in London, ever, but she did.

As soon as Anthony heard Paul's car horn in the street in the mornings, he ran down the two flights of stairs and was off to work looking very smart in his grey suit and wearing a tie. He hated formal business attire. The first thing he did when he arrived home in the evening was to shower and put on a pullover and casual trousers. He hated jeans; red was his preferred colour.

"I've had a terrible day. It was awful. I struggled so much to get the paperwork together for my residence permit. Every time I produced a document like a passport or a birth certificate, they asked for more documents plus photos. I'm sure they have shares in the automatic photo machine companies; I needed six. They gave me a list of official translators, as all my documents should get translated from English to French. It's going to cost me a tiny fortune. You really should take a day off work and come with me; it will be so much easier."

"No, no way, you can forget that idea. You'll learn the hard way by doing it alone, but you'll thank me in the end. You'll learn French quickly, and you'll also learn that you must count on nobody except yourself. This is a cruel world. I'm not going to help you with any administrative stuff either. I hate it, also because it's better for you to do it alone and lastly, I'm really lazy. I can't believe you didn't detect it already."

"You rat, I'm going to jump on your back and teach you a lesson."

They rolled around on the floor, and the friendly fight ended with sex on the rug. Lili did not take 'no' for an answer; this was his punishment.

The next day at eight o'clock, Lili's heart was beating ten to the dozen as she walked into the courtyard of the Alliance Française to start her lessons. There were foreigners of every colour and nationality. It was really noisy and smelled of French cigarettes. She felt lost and lonely, a real fish out of water, even though the majority of the foreign students were speaking in English amongst themselves, as English was the common language of the world. She nearly ran back to the metro station to go home. Instead, she pulled herself together, found some Dutch courage and walked into the registration office to be assigned a class after taking a short test, which unsurprisingly turned out to be a class for total beginners.

At ten o'clock, Lili was sitting in Madame Dupont's class on the first floor with twenty-three other foreign students. The majority were young Iranian women and Turkish men. There were also a few Dutch and Nigerian girls and some young Arab men. Lili was the only Brit from England. Curiously, there were no Americans. The whole two-hour session was in French. Madame Dupont only spoke French. The model for the course was based on everyday life in France around a French family. The tutorial book had pictures with phrases written underneath that the students had to repeat and learn parrot fashion. They were acquiring vocabulary and learning verbs. There were more hours of homework than classwork.

"My head feels like a sieve. I've been doing this homework since I finished a late lunch on a tray sitting on the sofa. Luckily, I did some shopping in the supermarket on my way home for tonight's dinner. I need a glass of wine; can you open the bottle, please? Perhaps you could help me with this homework or check what I've done after we've finished eating."

"I'll open the bottle, but I don't want you to think we're going to be drinking wine every night; it's not good for you, for us. Besides, the whole world has a false image of French people. The average family doesn't drink wine every day. Nor do we eat garlic with absolutely everything and have onion soup every night before going to bed. As for your homework, sorry, but I've no intention of helping you after I've had a hard day at work as well as a long drive back. Try to make friends quickly with your classmates and do homework with them before I get home, and then we can relax together."

"Well, well, well, thanks a million, thanks a lot for your great solidarity. You invited me to come to live in France with you, but you don't want to invest any energy in my integration and adaptation. Click your fingers, and hey presto, Lili will learn to speak French immediately and be completely autonomous. That's probably what you're thinking, but it's not going to be like that. It's going to be a long hard process, and we may not get to the end of it and still be together. You've really upset me; I'm off to bed. Good night."

The next day Lili went to make a phone call.

"Hello, Mum, I wanted to surprise you. I'm in the post office sending letters and cards to a few friends in London and wanted to have a chat with you. It's been a few weeks since we last spoke; how are you?"

"Lili! What a nice surprise. I'm fine, Luv. Ivy and I were just talking about you. Your ears must be burning. How are you?"

"I'm all right, thanks. I knew it wasn't going to be easy, but I didn't think it was going to be so hard. The life of a student isn't all it's made out to be; there is a lot of hard work. But I adore Paris. I've made some friends at the Alliance Française; after class, they come back to our flat, and we have working lunches. We speak English mostly because none of us speaks enough French to make any sense. Sometimes it's hilarious."

"And how's life with Anthony?"

"He's French."

"What does that mean?"

"Only that he's different to us Brits. Less laid-back and a bit arrogant. He's kind when he wants to be and likes to show me Paris, especially at weekends. We go to the old book shops in Saint Germain-des-Près and often walk along the river Seine and eat in some nice little Bistros. We've been to dinner and lunch a few times at his brother's and cousins' homes. They're so sweet and make me feel welcome. Anthony is a bit of an introvert. Before I change French courses and start at the Sorbonne in April for an accelerated course, what do you think about me visiting you in Chester for a few days and bringing Anthony? You have to meet him one day."

"Yes, of course, that's a great idea, it will be marvellous. If you give me your dates and flights, we'll pick you up from Liverpool airport. It'll be grand. I'll round-up the family, and we'll have some get-togethers. I could do some baking; do you think he'll like custard tarts and scones?"

"Mum, don't worry. As long as you serve him snails in garlic butter, sautéed frogs' legs, steak tartare and French fries, he'll be fine."

"God strewth, I've never eaten garlic in my life and have no idea where to buy it, let alone frogs' legs and serving raw beef, but I can easily do the chips."

"I'm pulling your leg. He's not fussy about his food and anyway, you're the best cook in the whole of England. Men would court you just to eat your scouse and fruit crumbles. The way to a man's heart is definitely through his stomach."

"Well, that's a relief then; you're terrible, always pulling my leg."

"Anthony wants me to go to the French Alps to meet his parents and teach me to ski. He says the snow can be good at this time of year. I told him he must meet my family first, so our visit is imminent."

"No problem, it's going to be lovely, and our Ivy already knows him. She's going to write to you this week. She was hired by the Cheshire County Police force, and can you believe they're paying for her to learn to drive? She looks smashing in her uniform and loves the job. Anyway, Ivy will tell you in her letter. Take care, Luv; we miss you to bits."

"Me, too, Mum. I can't wait to see you again. Just make sure you don't laugh too much in front of Anthony and make your false teeth fall out into the fireplace again."

"Grief! I'd forgotten about that incident, trust you, you've got a memory like an elephant's, don't you dare say a word to him about that, it was years ago. Ta-ra for now, Luv. I'm already looking forward to seeing you. God bless."

"We're going to be cut off any second now; I don't have any more franc coins to put in the phone box. Ta-ra, Mum, God bless."

It was Friday night, and Anthony usually returned home early on Fridays.

"*Bonsoir mon chéri*, I hope you had a good day. It will be great to have a sleep-in tomorrow, no Alliance Française or homework; I finished it with my friend Rosa, the Colombian girl. Guess what? I went to a local travel agent, got flight details and prices to fly to Liverpool next weekend. If you take Friday off, we could fly out from Orly at two o'clock after my lessons and arrive in Liverpool at two o'clock thanks to the one-hour time difference. Three days and two nights in England. What do you think?"

"I've never met any girl's mother in my life. It's going to be awful; can't we avoid it?"

"One day, you'll have to do it. The sooner, the better; get it over with. The following weekend or the one after, we can drive to the Alps for me to meet your folks and begin skiing."

"*D'accord* – Okay, let's book the trip tomorrow morning, and I forgot to tell you, we're invited to lunch with Paul. You can phone your Mum with the trip details from his flat. He's had a phone for years; lucky him."

Paul prided himself on being a good host, and he was. His elderly mother did all his shopping as usual. Paul's father died twenty-five years ago of a massive heart attack. Running errands for her only son kept her busy and made her feel useful. She really liked Lili and would have liked Paul to marry her. She thought Anthony didn't deserve Lili. Paul always served the same menu of foie gras and beefsteak with fried onions, followed by a generous cheese board, then a cake called Paris-Brest, named after the famous bicycle race from Paris to Brest on the Brittany coast. He always remembered how every guest liked his steak grilled.

While the men were talking business and setting the table like two old buddies, Lili phoned her mum to give the details about their arrival in Liverpool on Friday, in six days' time. Elsa-May said she was apprehensive about meeting Anthony; she had never had a foreign visitor in her home before, except for Uncle Chas, who was Welsh, but he could hardly be considered a foreigner. She told Lili that her eldest brother Lee would meet them and give a short-guided tour of the centre of Liverpool before driving over to Chester in the county of Cheshire through the river Mersey tunnel.

As usual, when Anthony was with Paul, she felt left out. Anthony ignored her. She often thought he was a misogynist. Lili had observed his behaviour on many occasions when he was in the company of women. He was often condescending, and she thought he believed she was inferior to him in more ways than one. She hoped things would go well with him and Elsa-May. One could walk on her toes, but not for long, she knew how to speak her mind, and she did.

Two months had passed since her arrival, and Lili started to understand French when she listened hard enough to conversations, watched TV and went to the cinema. She was still too shy to speak, except when it was absolutely necessary, like in the bank, the post office, the Town Hall for her resident papers and in the shops. However, she felt confident that one day she would speak like a native. Paul always spoke to her in French even though he spoke perfect English; she appreciated his encouragement because Anthony never spoke to her in French. Paul said she was progressing in leaps and bounds.

"Look, there's Lee waiting for us over by the cigarette machine. He's the tall bloke wearing glasses and the blue Everton FC football jacket. It's easy to see he's an ardent Evertonian. Our plane landed early, and he didn't see us coming through Customs. Let's walk over to him."

"Hey! Lili, look at you, our kid; you look great. You're still too skinny, though, but I like your purple coat. You're starting to look very Parisian."

"Thanks, thanks very much. I don't get many compliments these days. Lee, this is my boyfriend, Anthony; Anthony, this is my big brother Lee."

"Nice to meet you, Anthony. I'll shake your hand even though you're French, and we're supposed to hate each other if you read the history books."

"Don't listen to him. Lee has a weird Liverpudlian sense of humour, but he's harmless."

"I thought I'd take you and Anthony for a beer. In Liverpool, there's a pub on every street corner. I'm thirsty, and it's still 'opening time'. Afterwards, we could make a short tour of Liverpool city centre to show Anthony where your roots come from. Mum is in a real tiswas getting dinner ready and asked us to buy some wine and beers from the off-license for the meal."

After a pint of larger beer and a plate of beef and English-mustard butties and pork pies in the typical northern pub called The Beehive, they began their tour. The first stop, with Lee as their guide, was at one of the two Liverpool Cathedrals, officially known as The Cathedral Church of the Risen Christ. With its outside length of one hundred and eighty-nine metres, this Church of England cathedral, part of the Anglican Communion, is the longest cathedral in the world. Because of its overall inside volume, it is the fifth-largest cathedral in the world. It was constructed between 1904 and 1978 at the top of Saint James Mount. Anthony was truly impressed and took some photos with his mini-Canon camera. He got on like a house on fire with Lee, who he remarked was full of interesting anecdotes and useful information. The three bantered about and enjoyed each other's company. Lili was loving being back in Liverpool and England with her eldest brother, and she liked the way Anthony was relaxing.

As they didn't have a lot of time, they were only able to drive past the other cathedral; the splendid and atypical Catholic Cathedral officially called The Metropolitan Cathedral of Christ the King. The two cathedrals, being only half a mile apart, are linked by Hope Street, where the Royal Philharmonic Hall is located. The Irish people lovingly refer to the Catholic Cathedral as Paddy's wigwam or the Pope's launching pad because of its shape.

There are tens of thousands of Irish Catholics living in Liverpool. Around half a million arrived during the great Irish famine from 1845 to 1852, while thousands of others went to live in the United States of America. LJ, Lili's father, was a second-generation Irish Catholic. Lili had been christened in a Catholic church. Elsa-May changed religion from being Church of England to Catholic to be able to marry LJ in a Catholic church. LJ would never have converted. She was happy to have converted because she embraced the Catholic religion during the years of her married life. She changed back after the divorce but only to please her mother, who was an ardent Protestant. Elsa-May remained a Catholic at heart.

When they continued their tour after the cathedrals, they found a parking space in Lord Street in the centre and walked towards the waterfront. Lee was proud of his city, and he wanted to show Anthony the Three Graces: The Royal Liver building, The Cunard building and The Port of Liverpool Building, situated on Liverpool's Pier Head, lining the city's waterfront. The Pier Head is where the ferry boats cross the Mersey to Birkenhead and the Wirral areas and where boats sail out to the Irish Sea. It is assumed this group of buildings is named after the mythological Greek 'Three Graces', who were the daughters of Zeus, goddesses of charm, beauty and creativity.

Lee explained that the Liver building opened in 1911 and was purpose-built for the Royal Liver Assurance Group, which had been set-up in the city in 1850 to provide Liverpudlians with assistance if a wage earner lost his job. He said it was also one of the first buildings in the world built with reinforced concrete. The most recognisable landmark in the city, home to two fabled Liver birds called Bella and Bertie, half cormorant, half eagle. They are perched on the top of the building; one looks over the city, and the other out to sea. Legend has it that if the two birds fell, the city would burst its banks and cease to exist. Lee said he was sure the birds were really there to ensure that the pubs stayed open.

It was very cold, with the wind blowing up from the Irish Sea through the River Mersey and penetrating their bones. Lili suggested they drive over to Chester and visit the rest of Liverpool another time. She was in a real hurry to see her mother and sister.

Lili was the first out of the car knocking on the door of the big three-storey house on Watergate Street, inside the Chester walls, close to the Roodee race course- the oldest race course still in use in the United Kingdom of Great Britain, situated just a few yards outside the Chester walls.

Elsa-May, wearing a sky-blue woollen twin-set and tight skirt, answered the door with a big beaming smile. She was tickled-pink to see Lili looking so well and happy. Ivy ran down the stairs to greet them with a big Cheshire cat grin.

"OK, thanks, Anthony, you can go back to France now we've got our Lili back…ha-ha. You're both looking well. Did Lee's driving turn your hair grey?"

"Hello Ivy, you haven't changed. No, actually, I thought Lee drove very well, especially through the Mersey Tunnel. It's very strange for me to sit in a car that's driving on the other side of the road, the left side. This is my first visit to England."

"Come in then; nice to meet you, Anthony. You can call me Elsa-May; let's get out of the cold. Ivy will take you to the top floor with your bags. You'll have more privacy up there, and you'll have the use of the sitting room next to your bedroom and toilets. The electric blanket is on the bed. I hope we'll have a chance to play some board games and have a drink or two up there after dinner if you're not too tired from your journey and tour of Liverpool. I've roasted a chicken to be served with bread sauce, spuds and vegetables, followed by a homemade raspberry trifle. I hope you are hungry. Thanks for the wine."

"That's grand, Mum. Dinner smells delicious; we'll take our coats off, use the bathroom and be down in a jiffy. The weekend's going to fly by, and I plan on making each minute, no, every second, count."

Anthony was tired of trying to listen and join-in the all-English conversation; he went to bed at eleven o'clock. He had been cold in the bedroom without central heating, but he was now as snug as a bug in a rug in the large comfortable bed. He wanted to wait for Lili, but he knew she was dying to chat with Elsa-May alone. He entered the land of nod as soon as his head hit the feather pillow.

"Lili, you remember when I was angry with you for not marrying Jay when you first went to live with him in that garden flat in Hampstead? I just want you to know that I've changed; I don't want you to rush into any wedding with Anthony over in France. There's no need. Find a job and get financially independent. If it doesn't work out with him, you can always leave, no commitments, no lawyers. He seems to be a good man, but time will tell, you know what I mean!"

"Yes, of course, I know, a wedding is not on the cards. We've never spoken about marriage, don't worry. I'm not just a pretty face. I love this time of night when we sit together in front of the open fire sipping our mugs of hot chocolate, putting the world to right before going to bed. I love Paris and the challenge of what I'm doing. It's so different from living in London with Jay and being lonely. To be honest, I miss Jay, but the heartache is healing. I don't think I'll ever love another man as much as I loved Jay. There is someone for everyone, as they say, he was for me, but it didn't last. However, love at first sight exists, and I have experienced the fact."

Two weeks after their short trip to Chester, they hit the road to visit Anthony's parents in the French Alps, 375 miles away. From her passenger seat in the Lotus Elan, Lili was stunned by the amazing scenery as they came off the A6 motorway, known as the *autoroute du soleil* – the sunshine motorway. The road zig-zagged down the Mount Berthiand pass, 780 metres high in the Jura Mountain range, through the town of Nantua to the French Alps where Anthony's parents live. Following the road along its giant lake, through Bellegarde and another beautiful lake, they got near to the French Alps and Anthony's parents.

Anthony was concentrating hard, driving fast and was excited at the idea of going skiing the next day. He was a mountain man while Lili was a sea lover. She was an Island girl, of course, from the British Isles. She often described herself as such and usually got strange looks because her skin was not dark. She laughed, explaining she meant the British Isles, where the waters are cold, not warm. She could never be far away from a coastline for long periods. She needed to see seas and oceans and breathe the iodine. Whenever she felt melancholic and couldn't get to the coast, she went near a river or went swimming in a pool. That was her therapy and cure for everything.

"You are sweating."

"I know, it's the excitement and adrenalin. I could drive this road blindfolded; I know it so well. You are so occupied looking at the map and the scenery. We'll be on the road driving for another two hours."

"True, give me a map, and you'll never hear a peep out of me; this scenery is truly magnificent. You said we'd be in time for dinner; I wonder what your parents are thinking. I admit to being a bit nervous. You said they don't speak English and I haven't learnt enough French yet to be able to communicate properly. Don't leave me alone too long with them, and please translate as much as you can."

"You know very well I'm not going to do any translating; you'll just have to dive in at the deep end and fend for yourself. Body language is very important and will speak louder than words. My mother still can't believe I've got a girlfriend. It's going to be interesting to see her reactions. We'll shop tomorrow for your skis, ski shoes and a ski-suit to keep you warm. Thankfully we don't have to go far as we'll get them from my father's shop. He'll give us a family discount. Better be up early to get that done and try to be on the slopes at around ten o'clock. It's a good hour's drive up there to Flaine. We'll have breakfast at the ski resort and enjoy the sun coming up over the mountains. Let's try hard to get to bed on time."

"*Bonsoir mon fils* – Good evening my son."

Lili was introduced to Monsieur & Madame Beaumont. Madame was tall, blond, in her late sixties and would have been a very attractive woman in her youth. She was smoking with a cigarette holder and gave her hand to Lili to shake. Her husband was also tall but not as tall as Anthony, very slim, wearing sports clothes that made him look younger than his seventy years. He gave a formal greeting, but unlike his wife, he didn't smile.

They took their things to the guest room, and Lili suddenly felt very uncomfortable about sleeping with Anthony in his parents' house. Anthony just shrugged. The dinner was civil but not very convivial compared to Lili's family dinners. She could sense the father's disapproval. The homemade meal of vegetable soup with grated Tomme de

Savoy cheese, crusty whole-meal bread and a hot creamy rice pudding was delicious. Anthony told Lili his mother didn't cook as they had a housemaid that came in for a few hours every day. Monsieur Beaumont served a dry, fruity white wine from their Savoy region called Apremont as an aperitif before the meal. The conversation seemed to revolve around the parents' businesses and Anthony's eldest brother and his family, who lived an hour's drive away. Madame Beaumont never took her eyes off Lili, which made her fidgety.

'You should have seen the scene; it was comic. While you were in the bathroom, I was drinking a coffee with my father, and I told him we're getting married this summer. He nearly choked, and he called my mother, who nearly fainted. They congratulated me and said they think you're very nice and I'm a lucky man. My father will open his shop at seven o'clock to get you geared-up for skiing. All my things are in that big closet in the corner of the room."

"Anthony, why are you now hiding under the duvet? Stop laughing, and don't try to change the subject. You've lost your mind. Come up here, behave yourself. You could have proposed to me or discussed it with me first. I'm not even sure you're serious. You've never even said you love me. How can we get married if we don't love each other?"

"Bah, Lili, why not? Come here in my arms. We might as well, and it will be easier for you to live in France if you get French nationality. Thanks to our marriage, you can become naturalised."

"That's one way of looking at things. I don't think I could live permanently in any country where I couldn't vote for the people governing me and where I pay taxes, as well as not having the same nationality as my children."

"Let's make a baby tonight. It will be a Savoyard like me."

Monsieur Beaumont had already chosen some ski things for Lili. Anthony had given him her shoe size during dinner, and he'd been in the shop for over an hour. He showed them some blue, white and green compact skis and matching ski shoes for Alpine skiing, which fitted her perfectly; she liked the colours as well. She chose a green and white ski suit, a white woollen hat and gloves that coordinated with the rest of the gear and some anti-UV sun goggles. She was all set to go.

Monsieur Beaumont said she looked 'jolie' – pretty. Lili was really surprised at how sweet he was to her the morning after and how happy he looked, totally different from his attitude towards her during dinner the night before. She surmised he probably didn't have a good opinion of her when they arrived, thinking she was some promiscuous foreigner taking advantage of his son.

When Lili heard Anthony laughing, she got the gist that his father had phoned his eldest son Patrick and his wife Annabel, and they would have dinner together when they got back from skiing. Lili felt her stomach churn and crossed her fingers that she would be all right. Her nerves were in shreds. She didn't know what the devil had gotten into Anthony with his talk about a wedding.

They borrowed the parents' four-wheel-drive jeep as the small Lotus Elan would not make it through the snow on the mountain roads. The ski resort of Flaine was at 1600 metres and the top peaks were as high as 2500 metres. Anthony was happy driving up there with the snow tyres on the jeep; he knew they weren't going to risk having an accident. It had stopped snowing; the snow plough had left the road, and the sun was coming out. The scenery and surrounding mountains were breathtakingly beautiful. It was the first time ever that Lili had been on a ski trip; she started to relax and enjoy the views.

"Lili, you have to be more scared of me than the slopes and the mountain. If necessary, to make you ski down, I may have to tap you with my ski poles. Anyway, you have to get down this slope now that we're up here. You did fine getting on and off the chair lift, as well as practising the snow plough with your skis to help you stop in an emergency and to slow you down if you start picking up too much speed. You've got the knack of planting your ski poles in the snow in the direction you want to go and bending your knees... flexion, extension, flexion, extension. Be confident, stay close behind me, copy what I do and follow my tracks. I promise to go slowly and not do any fancy stuff. I've been skiing for twenty years, so I know what I'm doing and talking about. I want you to have fun, enjoy yourself, let yourself go and stop having that scared look on your face."

"I'm starting to hate you; you never told me I would be shaking in my boots with the fear of God in the pit of my stomach. Look how steep this slope is; I'll never be able to get down. I'm all dressed up like a dog's dinner in this outfit, but I'm freezing cold and have a sore bum from falling over all the time."

"OK, don't move. If you want to be a spoilt child, stay here in this spot. I'm going to ski down and get the chair lift back up again. I'm cold, and I need to do a fast run."

"Anthony, please don't leave me here. I'm sorry for what I said. Oh, dear Lord, he's already gone. It's exhilarating to be here in this valley, 2000 meters above sea level, I'm the lucky one, but I'm so bloody scared. Help!"

Anthony was back in no time. Lili followed him down as best she could, then went straight back up again. She didn't want Anthony to leave her a second time. Going up and down the green slope three times before lunch made Lili feel confident. She was also loving having the sun on her face and the wind in her hair. They relaxed on sun loungers on the terrace of the chalet restaurant after eating a tartiflette and smoked ham lunch with hot mulled wine.

Before they left the ski resort, Lili made a downhill run on a blue slope, the next hardest after the green slopes. She took the ski lifts and put her life in Anthony's hands. She was learning quickly and making progress, even if she did fall often. Anthony appeared to be proud of her, although he never said. He was not one to give her compliments; they were already a thing of the past.

Back at the parents' flat that evening, Lili was soaking in a bath of scented salts, relaxing with her eyes closed, thinking about the day. She felt exhilarated and couldn't believe she had managed to get through it and actually enjoyed the whole experience.

Madame Beaumont was setting the table for six. Maria, the housemaid, had prepared everything for them to have a Savoyard fondue. Anthony told her it was a popular meal of melted cheese from Haute Savoy, his mountain region, where the special cheeses are made from cows' milk. An iron pot is filled with three different types of cheeses in equal quantities: Beaufort, Comté and Emmental, melted in dry white wine in which pieces of baguette bread stuck on long sticks are dipped. The fondue can be served with local smoked hams and salad. Savoyard fondue is quite heavy to digest at night, but half way through the fondue, they will serve the famous Trou Normand – a Normandy hole, like we had at New Year at Flavie's, to help digest the cheese and make room for dessert.

Lili loved eating and trying new foods. Even if she would have preferred to climb into bed with a mug of hot chocolate, she was delighted to spend the evening eating fondue and meeting Anthony's brother. It had been a long day; she could already see and feel the bruises from her falls on the slopes. Early tomorrow, they would go to Morzine, another nearby ski resort. Anthony said it was nicer than Flaine. Flaine is in a closed valley, whereas Morzine is open, and the views over the mountain tops are even more spectacular. It was exciting. They said Patrick and his wife Annabel were sure to sleep over in the other guest room and go skiing with them.

"Your father is so generous and helpful; I like my skiing gear. It's unbelievable he didn't accept any payment. We're going to be tired later in the day, especially you at work, after our five-hour drive back from the Alps. We're mad, what an adventure; getting up at five o'clock on a Monday morning after an exhausting ski week-end, ah, but we only live once, and it was magic. I can't wait to go back and do it again. Annabel was a real gem; she gave me some good advice, and I progressed while you were trying to commit hara-kiri skiing off-piste on the edge of the slopes with Patrick. You're both really competitive, but I suppose that's because you are brothers. It grieves me to see you looking so miserable now. I realise how sad it must be for you to leave your mountains and be driving back to Paris."

"It certainly is. By the way, my mother said she would come to Paris, probably next month, to stay with my brother Jonathan and Claire. She misses them, especially her grandchildren. She wants to visit us, too, and talk about our wedding."

"Anthony, what wedding? There's no wedding. Hey, don't look at me; concentrate on the road. The traffic is getting dense as we're nearing Paris. You can drop yourself off at work, and I'll drive the rest of the way home. I've decided to skip school today and go back to bed; I can read my French books during the afternoon."

"All right, suits me. During the return journey tonight in Paul's car, I'll talk to him about our wedding and ask if he'll accept to be my Best Man."

"I can see you've got a one-track mind Monsieur Anthony Beaumont. When you've got an idea in your head, you can't be budged. Let's talk tonight."

A few weeks later, Lili said *au revoir* to her classmates at the Alliance Française during a round of drinks she bought at the cafe on the boulevard Raspail opposite the school and where they exchanged phone numbers to keep in touch after she began lessons at the Sorbonne Open University. Fortunately, their phone at home had been installed three days prior.

She revelled in the international atmosphere that reigned, with so many different cultures and languages. Learning and sharing cultures brought people together. Knowledge was power. They had spent many evenings eating and drinking together at different students' flats, each one bringing a typical type of food from his or her country and some wine. Music was also a way of breaking down cultural barriers. Of course, Lili always took some Beatles cassettes and brought music sheets with the lyrics for a sing-along. Everyone knew and liked the Beatles, didn't they?

Lili felt she couldn't go back to a one-language life style again. Anthony joined the multi-cultural gatherings, especially after the success of the one held in their flat. He danced to rock 'n' roll music with Lili. Madame Dupont turned up, and she wasn't the same person as the one in front of the blackboard at the Alliance Française. She was Niçoise from Nice and a very sunny person. Anthony went out of his way to find and serve cheese, bread and wines from Savoy and talked a lot about his wonderful region. The class was going to miss her, but it was only *au revoir* – see you again - not a good-bye.

Money was getting tight, Lili's savings were getting low, but she was receiving money each month from Jay as payment for all the things she had bought over the years and left in their flat in London, plus a nice premium from his company as she was the one and only share-holder with him. That would stop in August, Jay's company was doing well, and reading between the lines of his letters, he did love Lili universally. He was happy knowing she was enjoying her new life in France.

When her Sorbonne course finished in July, she did not want to rely completely financially on Anthony. She didn't want to be in that situation; she had always paid her own way and was ferociously independent. There was no doubt Lili had to continue her lessons to read, write and speak French correctly, even perfectly, then get a job.

Madame Beaumont had insisted on giving Lili and Anthony a big cheque to open a savings account as a deposit to buy a home. She was totally against renting and throwing money out of the window, as she said. However, she liked their rented flat and obviously appreciated Lili, and her second son was at last living with a woman, his fiancée, and planning for the future. Madame Beaumont gave Lili her own sapphire and diamond engagement ring during the Easter Sunday lunch in Paris. She knew Anthony thought it totally ridiculous to buy jewellery. Lili was very moved, nearly to tears. It was impossible to refuse; Madame Beaumont did not take no for an answer. Now it seemed impossible to refuse to marry Anthony. He looked very chuffed.

On the 1st of April, an unusually hot spring day, Lili's lessons began at the Sorbonne right after the Easter break. Again, like at the Alliance Française, there were students of all ages and nationalities in her class. She immediately struck a friendship with three English girls around her own age, Paige, Sharon and Lisa. They looked like fun and turned out to be terrific friends. Lili hadn't realised how much she missed the English sense of humour. Unlike Lili, they were only in Paris for the spring and summer, just for the experience and the joys of living in Paris, of which there were many, before going back to England to pick-up their lives unless they came across a French prince charming to sweep them off their feet. But, as Paige said, you have to kiss a lot of frogs before finding a prince charming. Well, they were in France, the best place to be for that; the odds were on their side.

Mademoiselle Moreau was a young and attractive teacher who, like Madame Dupont, only spoke French. They were expected to learn the whole of the thick red French book they had been issued that contained everything they needed to learn the French language and some French culture before taking an exam in July. For a few days, the four young English women sat together in front of the big window but were inevitably separated. Mademoiselle Moreau could see they were trouble. Lili was assigned to sit between Tokay, a thirty-four-year-old Turkish man with a thick black moustache who had arrived in Paris from Istanbul to open a restaurant in the Pigalle district, and Gilda, a big blond German woman about thirty years old who moved to Paris to live with her French boyfriend whom she had met on holiday in Cannes a year ago.

Paige was put in the front row in the middle of two nineteen-year-old Finnish twins. Sharon was put at the back next to Stu, short for Stuart, a stocky American guy with a big orange beard covering his chin who said he was forty-five years old but turned out to be only twenty-seven. He was actually an interesting, handsome dude. He knew so much about French literature and gave Lili titles of books to read by authors such as Gustave Flaubert, Honoré de Balzac and Albert Camus. She read them first in English, then bought the original French version in paperback. Stu had been in France for a number of years and had taken a few courses, mostly art and literature. He understood and spoke French fairly well; it didn't make sense for him to be in their intermediary class. But, although he didn't say it, they guessed it was to avoid being drafted into that terrible, senseless war in Vietnam.

Lisa was happy to remain seated near the window next to Abru, a young Iranian girl in her twenties who insisted on being called Persian, not Iranian.

Lili found it much harder at the Sorbonne, especially as the hours were longer, from nine to four o'clock with an hour for lunch instead of ten till twelve at the Alliance Française. The work was difficult, they conjugated verbs in all tenses, including the subjunctive, which doesn't exist in English.

Paige and the other girls didn't worry too much about the grammar, they didn't need to, but Lili did. They had picnic lunches in the Luxembourg gardens or walked down the boulevard de Montparnasse stopping to have snacks and coffee before returning to the class. They went out together some evenings, mostly to bars and cafés. Sometimes Paige and Sharon didn't go to class; they went shopping or did tourist things. Lili, nose to the grindstone, was unable to give herself that luxury yet.

Paul stopped going out with Anthony in the evenings since Lili's arrival in Paris. She didn't know why and Anthony never explained, even though she could see he was sad and put-out. Lili left Anthony home alone in the evening about twice a week, and that suited him fine. He needed some peace and quiet.

One afternoon after class, the girls took a bus with Paige to the flat where she lived on the top of a magnificent building on the Quays overlooking the Louvre Museum. A family friend had brought Paige some English sausages, bacon, baked beans and crumpets back from England. Paige wanted to share them because she knew that her British friends were totally unable to live without them for a long period. They tasted and smelt so good; the girls were really in high spirits afterwards, with their stomachs bulging.

While waiting at Paige's flat for Stu the American and Tokay the Turk to arrive to go with them to listen to an English band play in a bar near the George Pompidou Centre on the other side of the river Seine, Paige spotted them down below in the street nearing the door. She quickly ran to the fridge to get some eggs and dropped them out of the window, then hid behind the curtains. It was typical of her daring nature and totally hilarious; they all fell about laughing. Stu was furious, he was ranting and raving when he got up to the flat, but he never found out who did it. Paige was lucky the eggs landed just in front of him and Tokay, not on their heads, or they might have been seriously injured.

A big event was the arrival of Sofia in Paris, Paige's eldest sister. Apart from being fluent in French, she was very chic and mature for her twenty-five years. Paige was lovely, too, in a more casual style, with long dark hair and mischievous brown eyes. Paige introduced Sofia to the group. Shortly after, she started going out with Stu. Sofia was working as the personal assistant to Cassandra, the owner of the famous perfume shop opposite the Hotel Inter-Continental on the corner of rue de Rivoli and rue de Castiglione. She did all her correspondence and answered an incredible amount of foreign phone calls. Cassandra was the most famous perfume shop in Paris, next to the hotel

Meurice and close to the hotel Ritz. Very glamorous wealthy tourists bought their perfumes and gifts from Cassandra, even movie stars and famous people. Cassandra always gave a big discount, and staff packed and shipped perfumes all over the world, mostly to North America and Canada. Lili liked Sofia and hoped they would stay friends when Paige returned to London at the end of summer.

Lili was thankful she and Anthony had bought a big convertible sofa. It was becoming indispensable for the mass of visitors coming and going to the flat. The first visitors were her brother Rod with one of his best friends at the start of their bike-trip across Europe. As it turned out, they didn't stay long in France before heading to Italy and Greece. They complained all the roads in France had been built by Romans and were far too straight and boring.

Sister Ivy came a few times. She was earning a good salary at the police force. She didn't want to see Paul again or do anything special with Anthony. She just wanted to go out with Lili and her friends. She thought Anthony was condescending, and she had a hunch he didn't like her very much; no love was lost.

Sadly, cousin Jen never visited Lili in France. To everyone's surprise, she married Dan, a bloke she had only known for a short time after she left Pete. Lili made a promise to visit her in Liverpool as soon as an opportunity arose. It was well known that Dan kept Jen on a close reign and was very possessive. Lili remembered all the great times they had together and how it was thanks to Jen she had met her ex-boyfriend, Jay.

The most surprising visit was from Olivia, the wife of Igor, from her office in London. Olivia came with arms full of useful and practical items, including a pressure cooker. Olivia adored two things; shopping and going to Tea Rooms. It was inevitable that they went to the two best-known ones, Angelina on the rue de Rivoli opposite the Tuileries gardens and Ladurée on the avenue des Champs-Elysées. Nobody made better macaroons than Ladurée, founded in 1862, and Olivia swore they must still be as good. Despite their ridiculous price, they ate three each with pots of Darjeeling and Earl Grey tea. Olivia preferred the lavender, pistachio and vanilla flavours.

Once, Olivia was gloomy on the drive back to Orly airport and told Lili how much she was missed. Igor had instructed Olivia to tell Lili that she could have her job back if she wanted. Lili was touched and sincerely flattered and promised to visit Olivia and Igor in London as well as the office, but going back to live in London was not an option. Paris was her home.

One evening in the middle of the week, much to Lili's surprise, Anthony suggested they go for a drink on the top floor of the Montparnasse tower and eat afterwards at a small Bistro they had once tried on the avenue de Maine, a stone's throw away from the tower. She soon found there was a method in his madness. He wanted to talk seriously about their wedding. He knew she couldn't escape the topic once they had been seated in the restaurant.

Lili believed she could never love another man more or better than she had loved Jay. She was never going to marry Jay. It was too late; he was the ship that had passed in the night. She did love Anthony, but it was a different kind of love, incomparable. *Compare the comparable*, she thought. Anthony, using all his French charm, looked at her in such a way all her resistance tumbled down.

They decided on a date in late August for a civil ceremony, followed by a fortnight's honeymoon in Scotland. Anthony loved old Scotch whiskeys and wanted to visit a few distilleries. A colleague had told him that a part from golfing at Saint Andrew's, fishing salmon was one of the best sports in Scotland. You could give the fish you caught to be smoked, and they posted them to you in an overnight special cold-sealed package. Lili had been all over England,

Ireland and Wales but never to Scotland. She thought it was a great idea.

Lili flew into Liverpool for a four-day long weekend. Ivy met her and proved once again to be a little gem. The minute it was open, Lili went to the Registrar's office in Chester to fix the date for the civil wedding ceremony. Ivy helped with everything, including the choice of the wedding dress, accessories, flowers, the venue for the wedding banquet, hotels and transport for out-of-town guests. The date was fixed, and the invitations were printed in English and French. Lili spent a morning with a travel agent to book accommodation in The Lakes and some cities and towns in Scotland, including Loch Ness, to see the monster, she wished! There were still umpteen things to do, but they could be done by phone calls or letters from France,

Lili was happy and high on adrenalin when she got back to Paris. From the airport, Anthony took her directly to the jeweller to buy the wedding rings from one Paul recommended, two simple matching eighteen-carat white gold rings that were perfect for him and her.

Her friends at the Sorbonne gave a surprise party one evening at Paige's flat when they heard the news of the forthcoming August wedding.

Lili was taking her French lessons and studies very seriously and enjoying every minute of the time spent in the Sorbonne in-between finalising the wedding arrangements.

"Hi, Anthony; I'm home. Why are you sitting completely still in the dark?"

"I am not well; I have a headache and feel sick."

"Oh Lord, Anthony, I think we should phone a doctor. Perhaps you've got summer flu."

"No, stop fussing; I'll be fine. Tomorrow's Saturday, I'll have the whole weekend to recover."

"Do you think we'll still go to Paul's for brunch tomorrow?"

"No, definitely not; it's cancelled. He told me today his boss is sending him on a three-year assignment to Washington, DC. He will fly out as soon as his visa is issued. You can imagine all the preparations. Obviously, this puts a damper on our wedding. He will be too busy in his new job to take time off to go to England. I cannot count on him to be my Best Man."

"Oh hell, never mind, but it is a shame you were looking forward to him being there holding your hand, figuratively speaking. If you like, I'll ask my friend and ex-boss, Igor. He speaks perfect French and loves ceremonies."

"OK, that could be an alternative, I've only met him twice, but you are right. He's a great personality and would be perfect in the role. I feel shocked about Paul's announcement; I admit it has shaken me, and his absence will leave a gaping hole in my professional and personal life. I'll have to find another person to share the commute to work. I'm already sick of it all."

"I'll write to Igor tonight and phone him and Olivia next weekend when we stay with your parents in the Alps. Remember, they want us to spend a couple of days to brief them about the wedding arrangements and to make a wedding gift list for family and friends. Your brother Patrick wants to get involved in the arrangements and help you choose your outfit. It's a pity he doesn't speak English. Anyway, this morning I went to pick-up the over-night train tickets for the journey instead of driving; it's all set. Thinking about it, I'm sure Igor and Olivia will be delighted. Take heart, Darling, for goodness' sake, get a grip!"

Anthony was inconsolable and became morose. Lili was worried and phoned Paul to tell him, but that didn't help. Paul did not understand why Anthony was making such an issue about his assignment to The United States of America. He congratulated Lili on passing her Sorbonne exam and getting her diploma. He wanted to hear about her plans to find work. She told him first things first, the wedding, then a job.

Paul shook hands with Anthony and gave Lili a hug when they were separating at the airport. He had lots of excess baggage when checking-in for his direct flight to Washington, DC. Paul was glad they had accompanied him to the airport in his Peugeot and was happy to give the car to them to use during his absence, knowing they would keep it serviced and safe in their underground car park.

Lili thought Anthony looked like death warmed-up and told him on the way home. He never replied or spoke and stayed in a bad mood for over a week. *Such is the life,* she thought.

Looking at the white cliffs of Dover when arriving on the shores of England always made Lili feel proud. That happened every time when crossing the English Channel from Calais to Dover on the car ferry. She imagined throughout history the many kings, queens, sailors, crusaders, perhaps even Christ, amongst others, who had all seen those giant white cliffs, reminding them of England's greatness.

Charles Hubert Parry's music to William Blake's famous hymn known as 'Jerusalem' came to her mind:

"And did those feet in ancient time walk upon England's mountains green, and was the holy Lamb of God on England's pleasant pastures seen. I will not cease from mental fight, nor shall my sword sleep in my hand, 'till we have built Jerusalem in England's green and pleasant land."

Had Jesus Christ really been to England as a youth to visit the town of Glastonbury, Somerset, where he established a second Jerusalem, as some said? She would never know, but those were wonderful words. Lili loved England.

Anthony and Lili disembarked the car ferry in Dover to drive the long road up north to Chester. They would be married in three days' time. The night before, in their big bed in Paris, they had made love. It had been long and slow, good for both of them. Lili needed reassurance and needed to know she was doing the right thing by marrying Anthony. She liked his slim, long and muscular body. She always got her way; he never refused her. He understood her libido and liked to lie in her arms afterwards, his mind far away.

There was such chaos in her mother's house upon arrival. It was full of neighbours, friends, family, early-arrived English guests; you name it. Anthony felt like a fish out of water and was confused by everything that was going on. Lili was glad she had booked them into the hotel Riverside by the River Dee for the three nights prior to the wedding. She was going to return to Elsa-May's house the night before the wedding and leave Anthony in the hotel room alone, as tradition demanded.

The Beaumont family arrived in Chester in the early afternoon of the day before the wedding. Their journey had been very long and tiring from the Alps to Paris to catch a flight to Liverpool, where they were met by a hired mini bus driven by a chauffeur. They adored Chester and went sightseeing with Anthony after dropping their bags off at the hotel Riverside. Suddenly, they were no longer tired, and the weather was hot and sunny. They had brought their brollies for nothing as they thought that English summers did not exist.

The Beaumont family met Lili's for the first time, and there was an unmistakable 'entente cordial'. Their different languages were no barrier. With the help of her friends, Elsa-May had prepared a typical English buffet in the large dining room on the ground floor of their home on Watergate Street. The Beaumont family helped themselves to salmon and cucumber sandwiches, deviled eggs, sausage rolls, meat pies with water cress, potato and beetroot salad, sliced roast beef, sliced York ham, salad, crisps, trifle and apple tarts. Ivy helped her brother Lee to serve some real English ale and

French wines; it was a very happy gathering. Also present around the table were Lili's ex-boss, Igor, in the role of Anthony's Best Man, with his wife Olivia and Pauline and Reg, her London neighbours and close friends. Pauline was heavily pregnant and looked really well. The two couples had arrived together and were the life and soul of the gathering. Anthony was jovial and seemed happy being the centre of attraction for once.

Lee was proud to be playing the role of giving his sister Lili away to Anthony the following day in place of LJ, their father. LJ had not been told about Lili's wedding simply because they didn't know where he lived or how to get in touch with him anymore.

Lee, her eldest brother, who had been the head-boy prefect in their college, and played the double bass during assembly, always kept a brotherly eye on Lili. It was typical of Lee to learn and play such an unusual and very cumbersome instrument; his choices were unusual. He was atypical and so utterly unique.

True to himself, Lee loved fishing and would go off on Sundays with his bucket and fishing rods to catch perch in the local rivers. He gave names to each fish he caught and brought home to put in his fishing pool in the family garden, the one he had created. Their names all began with the letter

P. The one he never brought home but caught time after time was Percy. He loved Percy. But he loved his football team, even more, Everton FC, his passion. From the age of twelve, he woke at six o'clock every morning, three hundred and sixty-five days a year, to deliver milk to houses before going to school. The money he earned paid for his season ticket for Everton FC's home games at Goodson Park and bus-coach fares and entrance fees to watch their away games all over the country.

Lee gave some of his earnings to Elsa-May to help out. He was noble in thought and deed. Elsa-May trusted him to look out for himself and also for her youngest son, Lee's brother, Rod, who went with Lee later on when he was twelve years old and also did a milk round for the same dairy-produce shop, and for the same reason. They became competitors as the years went by, such different characters, but they would always agree on one thing; Everton FC was the best football club in the United Kingdom of Great Britain.

Lili woke early on her wedding day, opened the curtains and lay in bed alone, admiring the sky and the view of the Welsh Hills in the distance and thinking about the day ahead. She could see her beautiful white dress hanging on the outside of the wardrobe and could smell coffee brewing, grilled bacon and toast. Ivy brought her some breakfast on a tray.

"Here comes the bride, here comes the bride... Good morning the future Madame Beaumont. How are we feeling on this special day? Here's some breakfast to keep you going until you say, "I do"."

"Thanks, Luv. I've been wide awake since seven o'clock, remembering that just over a year ago, we were in Paris together, where I met Anthony and today, I'll be marrying him, my prince charming. It seems like a fairy tale. I'll be living on the Continent and speaking French. So much has happened in just one year. I've learned the basics of a new language, learnt how to ski, made oodles of new friends and have a new man for better or worse for the rest of my life."

"Yeah, I hope it will be for better rather than worse. It's amazing; who would have thought?"

To keep you updated, the phone and the doorbell haven't stopped ringing since I got out of bed this morning. After you went to tuck Anthony in his hotel bed last night, our cousin Jen with her husband and a few others, arrived in town. They came here this morning and are now downstairs having breakfast with Mum. The flowers have been delivered as well as the three-tier cake for the restaurant.

Mum has planned a buffet meal here tonight with all the guests who can continue the celebrations after you leave on honeymoon, plus some of Mum's personal friends and neighbours. Rod is already helping Lee organise the music, the bar and the limos to take us to the Registry office, the restaurant and back here again.

"Crikey Ivy, what would I do without all of you? Especially you; you're such a brick."

"You're right, I know; you're so lucky to have us! Seriously, Lili, but Anthony takes it all for granted and behaves as if it's his due for us to run around after him. He hasn't lifted a finger to help with any of the organisation or arrangements. I hope you know what you're letting yourself in for. Start as you mean to go on instead of treating him like a kid."

"I know it's a bit off, but I think you'll agree that his parents, brothers, sisters-in-law, nieces and cousins who have come all this way from France for the event are really nice, and I'm lucky to have such a wonderful family-in-law."

"Yes, you're right, but they're lucky to have you, too. It cuts both ways."

"I hear what you're saying; thanks for the advice. I had better eat this scrummy breakfast, then bathe and get ready. See you downstairs for the 'off'."

Lili arrived with Lee at the Registry office exactly on time, feeling nervous and looking lovely. Everyone crowded around, giving compliments, strangely, all except Anthony. He never said a kind word. He looked dashing, as they say, in a dark pin-striped suit and grey bow tie. Ivy, as Lili's witness and bridesmaid, was dazzling, her long blond hair curled down her back, wearing a long light green Laura Ashley off-the-shoulder cotton dress. Elsa-May wearing a large brimmed yellow hat was hiding a tear as the first of her offspring was about to get married. She had spent little time with Lili during the past few days; she kept herself very busy to avoid thinking about what was happening, that Lili was going back to the Continent, probably forever.

During the photo session after the ceremony, on the steps of the Chester walls in front of the river Dee, close to the restaurant, a big white tomcat refused to go away. Elsa-May was shooing it off with all her might, but it kept coming back, sitting on the wall, walking around and strutting its backside. It was comic, but Elsa-May was convinced it was bringing bad luck. It was not a good omen.

Chapter Ten

THE HONEYMOON

"You've made your bed; now you must lie in it."

Lili mumbled to herself. This time there was no getting away from it. This was her honeymoon, her first night as Madame Beaumont!

Lying in bed late at night with Anthony sleeping beside her, she quietly sang the lyrics to that Beatles song she knew so well, entitled 'If I give my heart to you'. It always pulled at her heartstrings. She was feeling like a newly-wedded bride, despite herself and her situation, in their bridal suite at the Royal Crown Hotel in the Lakes. She stopped singing that nostalgic song and, with lots of gusto, changed to 'We can work it out', and she was ready to believe it.

"No use crying over spilt milk," Lili said to no one in particular. She looked at her groom in the queen bed, sleeping after only giving her a peck on the cheek. His dull excuse for not making love to his bride was tiredness after the events of the day. It had certainly been a long drive to The Lakes from Chester, where their civil marriage ceremony had taken place in the Registry Office. Tonight, they were spending their first night together as Monsieur & Madame Beaumont.

Lili was dog-tired. She turned off the bedside light and cuddled up to Anthony, her husband, and thought: *tomorrow is another day and the first day of the rest of my life.*

The next morning bright sunlight streamed through the half-open curtains onto their faces. Anthony was the first to wake up at the sound of the phone ringing on his side of the bed.

"Wake up, Lili, the phone is ringing. It's nearly ten o'clock, and we're going to miss breakfast.'

"Well, answer it yourself."

"I don't know who it is. If it's your Mum, don't tell her or anyone that we didn't make love last night, it will be so embarrassing for me as a Frenchman not living up to his reputation as a Latin lover."

"Oh, sod off, nobody else cares about that except me. I was really lonely and sad when you were sleeping."

"Hello, Mum. Yes, thanks, we had a very good journey, the hotel and the Lakes are everything we hoped for, really nice. We're going to eat breakfast and have a lazy morning. Thank you for everything you did to make the wedding a great success. You're such a gem. Anthony said he was sorry about us rushing off the way we did, leaving all the guests with you and the others to entertain, especially as most of them came a very long way. I feel terrible about it. Tell me how it all turned out when we get back to Chester in a fortnight. I'll phone you in a couple of days, must dash to the breakfast room. Ta-ra, Mum, God bless."

"Let's dress quickly and run down the stairs; I'm starving."

When they left Paris to drive to England, there had been an unbearable heat wave somewhere in the high thirties celsius. In the Lakes, it was only 10°celcius. Lili had thought it unnecessary to pack a coat, thinking there would be no need. She only had summer clothes and one cardigan. Anthony was smirking, wearing long trousers, and a long-sleeved shirt with a pullover and jacket. Happy not to have trusted the British climate even in summer. He especially did not trust Scottish weather further north. The long meandering walks in the countryside and pretty towns with stops at cafés to drink hot tea and coffee to keep them warm soon made up for the appallingly cold but sunny weather. They prayed it would get better, but as Murphy would have it, it got worse.

The couple left England and entered Scotland, heading directly for Edinburgh, the capital of Scotland, on the East

Coast, where they knew the annual Edinburgh International Festival was taking place and had been since 1947. Lili copiloted and planned the journey; she loved reading maps and travelling, giving a running commentary about this place and that on the way. They would go to Saint Andrew's by sea and through Cairngorms National Park onto Loch Ness and Inverness in the North. They would fish in rivers, buy some tartan from the mills, drink whiskey in the distilleries and pubs, eat haggis in restaurants, Angus steak in the best hotels, buy some wellies and raincoats if necessary and hopefully make love. Life was good, and the future looked promising. But, as fate would have it, Murphy was still lurking.

It was so cold in their hotel perched on top of one of the hills in Edinburgh they spent the whole time fully clothed and wrapped in quilts. The wind was howling, and the rain dripped onto the floor from the holes in the window frames. *It couldn't get any worse*, Lili thought. They wanted to change hotels, but as it was the yearly International Festival, there were no vacant rooms anywhere. The city's population of four hundred and forty-one thousand practically doubled during the festival period in August. As they had not booked any shows or concerts beforehand, they were disappointed not to be able to get any tickets for the ones they wanted.

"Let's leave the city tomorrow. There are too many people here, even if we do recognise and rub shoulders with some well-known actors, artists and singers in the streets. It's a great place; we'll come back another time, but out of season."

"OK, Lili, you're right, *on y va* - let's go."

Loch Ness was a flippin' wash out; the mist was so thick they could only make out the shape of the Loch from their car parked on the roadside, and no boat would take them out for a ride. They bought a few bottles of twelve-year-old whiskey after tasting it in a distillery near Inverness and drank some in the hotel bedroom until they fell into a deep sleep. St Andrews was their favourite place, named after Saint Andrew the Apostle, and known worldwide as 'the home to golf'. Neither of them had ever tried playing golf, but they loved St Andrews, the one place where the sun had shinned. The St Andrews white sandy beach was amazing. Wearing a one-piece bathing suit, Lili tried to swim in the sea, but the North Sea was too cold, even for her, even for anyone.

They were glad to see the family again when they got back to Chester. It was understandably hard saying goodbyes and returning to France on the car ferry, but at least in Paris, the weather was blissfully warm. The beautiful wedding gifts had been shipped to them during their honeymoon. They wanted for nothing; they were blessed.

One of Lili's hobbies was reading and studying astrology and zodiac signs, especially Chinese zodiac signs. She was born in the year of the rabbit, or the year of the cat, as the Vietnamese say. Vietnam has no rabbits in its lunar calendar, so she thought she would always land on her feet. She felt feline, and even her eyes had a feline shape. According to her zodiac sign, her triangle of friendship was with goats and pigs. Anthony was born in the year of the goat; they made a good match! She wished and hoped it was true.

After settling back into Parisian life, Lili realised with horror that her fun-loving friend Paige had gone back to live in London after passing her diploma from the Sorbonne and celebrating her twenty-first birthday at the fabulously posh restaurant La Tour d'Argent. Some of the other students had returned to their different countries or were in other parts of France.

The good news was that Sofia, Paige's sister, was still there. She invited Lili to lunch in her flat overlooking the Tuileries gardens. The bad news was that Sofia was also going back to London to work in the family firm. She knew Lili wanted to work, especially in a French environment, to practice what she had learned at the Sorbonne. Sofia had spoken to her boss, Cassandra, at the perfumery about Lili replacing her. Lili was flabbergasted but thought it was a great idea and a wonderful opportunity. The appointment to meet Cassandra was already fixed. Sofia was sure everything was going to be fine, which it was.

A month later, Lili found herself alone upstairs in the small open office overlooking the crowded perfumery below. Cassandra certainly had an amazing international clientele, mostly comprising rich Americans who couldn't spend their dollars fast enough on expensive perfumes such as 'Joy' by Jean Patou. It was his first creation, launched in 1929, made from exceptional ingredients. Joy was the most expensive perfume in the whole world, and Jean Patou has been deemed the best perfume creator ever.

Lili had worked with Sofia for the handover period and felt comfortable as the PA to Cassandra, who was friendly but demanding. Every day was different, never boring. Cassandra had an address book that even Royalty would be proud to possess. She thought the hours from ten to six o'clock with an hour for lunch suited her perfectly, and the perfumery was eight direct metro stops away from home. Listening and speaking French with fellow passengers, customers and staff was paying off; she had, at last, started to feel comfortable in crowds with the language.

However, after the first few weeks, she realised there were not enough days in her weeks to accomplish all of Cassandra's demands; the job was more challenging than she had imagined. She thought she ought to hire Mary Poppins to handle the heavy load. Uncannily she had thought that, not long after Julie Andrews, who played the role of Mary Poppins in the Walt Disney productions film, walked through Cassandra's door. As it happened, Julie was one of Cassandra's best and favourite clients. Lili wanted to chuckle and tell Anthony about the coincidence, but she didn't because she was tired when she got home late, which was often these days. She never left before seven o'clock then there was the metro journey home. Anthony was in a bad mood once again; his moods were a continuous source of friction between them.

Fortunately, they did enjoy a good social life with family and friends that made things bearable, except for the Paul issue, whose absence seemed much too hard for Anthony to contend with. They went as often as they could at weekends to practice archery at Anthony's Godfather's summerhouse in the countryside south of Paris. Her bow, bought at Le Vieux Camper, one of their favourite sports equipment shops in the heart of the Latin Quarter, had a 26 lb. pull. She loved the sport and became proficient after much practice; archery also helped alleviate her lower back problems and kept her fit.

Lili adored new experiences; she was learning to windsurf on a lake west of Paris. A few years later, on holiday, they took the windsurfer and crossed the English Channel on a hovercraft to Brighton, then drove down the coast to meet her brothers and their partners for a holiday in a rented cottage. After falling off the first time in the cold English waters, she dashed off to buy a wet suit. Her brothers pulled her leg, saying she was becoming nesh just like the Continentals.

Brother Lee had also married, and his wife was expecting their first baby. She was going to be an Auntie for the first time on her side of the family. She was happy for her brother; she was sure he was going to be a great dad but sad for herself while looking at her sister-in-law's bulging belly. Lili never used any form of contraception, but nothing was happening. She and Anthony had consulted doctors and made some tests. There was no physical reason to stop them from becoming parents.

Lili made another appointment to talk to Dominique, her gynaecologist, who had also become a friend. Dominique asked if everything was all right between her and Anthony, saying that often it's a mental thing with women who don't conceive because the little voice in their heads tells them not to conceive if things are not right. Lili was feeling morose and melancholic, thinking that something was missing in their marriage and relationship. Theirs was a threesome, an extra person that should not be there, albeit invisible for the most part. For the first time, she decided to confide in someone, Dominique.

"I've taken stock of my life with Anthony and thought about everything very carefully. On the one hand, I care about him and adore my French in-laws, all of them, and I would not want to stop seeing them. I enjoy financial comfort thanks to both our salaries. We have holidays in the sun in summer and ski clubs or resorts in the winter. I love the way we dance together at parties. I like to mother Anthony, and he needs to be mothered. But, on the other hand, I hate his possessiveness, sulking, distant and unreachable moody behaviour. I once asked him if he was in love with his friend Paul. I know he is, he would never admit it, but he doesn't deny it. He has never said he loves me; he just thinks I'm his wife. Personally, I don't need to be married to have an identity. I know who I am, and I feel something is definitely missing!"

"Well, you know, Lili, things have a way of working themselves out. If there's a solution, you'll find it, so don't worry. If there isn't, you'll move on in time, so don't worry. You are young and healthy; try to relax and go on a holiday."

Time to move on, thought Lili. Working for Cassandra is not bad, but it's not a career. There's nothing more I can learn and no ladder to climb. All my colleagues are much older than me and have been employees for yonks. Either I quit and go on a long journey, live the dream, or I apply for a job in one of the many international corporations located in Paris before I start a family. Hah, starting a family would be a fine thing.

"Is your steak tartare seasoned enough?"

"*Oui,* - yes, tastes fine."

"Preparing that is quicker than cooking after work, and I know you enjoy it. Anthony, I'm going to leave Cassandra's; my mind is made up. I'll tell her on Friday - TGIF - Thank God it's Friday - she will have the weekend to think about who she can find to replace me. It's a dead-end. I've been there for two years. I plan to register with a couple of temp agencies and do some replacements to see if there's anything out there that could suit me better. After my notice period and before temping, let's go on holiday now that the summer season is approaching. A holiday will be good for both of us."

Anthony had passed his permit *mer hauturier* – full sea-going boat license - the year before on the Marne River, east of Paris, which meant he could captain a big sailing boat with an engine or any type of boat with a motor. They had gone to the Marne on Saturdays for six consecutive weeks and had spent days on the practice boat. They loved the walks along the river Marne and ate out at one of the popular 'guinguettes' – open-air cafés with a dance area - where people came and went, dined and danced. The scene was one of a French impressionist painting, like Renoir's. Anthony was at ease and liked those outings and surroundings. He thought they could hire a boat in the south of France and sail over to the Island of Corsica and then around it before sailing back along the Italian and French Rivieras to the Côte d'Azur.

Of course, he said, seas are not comparable to mountains. Quoting what Lili often said that one should compare the comparable, but he liked sailing. After reflection, he intended to rent a catamaran for their sailing holiday.

He explained to her that catamarans have double cabins in the hulls, each with a shower and toilet. They are very stable and have natural buoyancy, making them unsinkable. Catamarans can capsize in a bad accident, but it's better to be rescued floating on the water's surface than sinking to the bottom of the sea in a monohulled boat. Moving around on a catamaran's flat deck is safer than on a deck at an angle like on single hulls.

He had searched and found some catamarans advertised for rent in Port Grimaud in the South of France near Saint-Tropez, or Saint-Trop, as the locals and the Tropezians called the town.

They needed at least one other couple to join them to help share the expenses plus the manoeuvrings and the shift-watches day and night. They thought about their good English friends Sally and James, childless as themselves. As luck would have it, they were free and up for the fun and challenge of sailing together for fifteen days in the Mediterranean Sea, known as 'the big blue'.

Feeling light-foot and fancy-free upon their arrival in the Côte d'Azur – The French Riviera – in the South of France, on the overnight couchette train, they took a taxi to the boat rental office in Port Grimaud. The bright blue cloudless sky, palm trees and warm sea breeze made a big contrast to what they had left behind in Paris. The Cat was great, an Iroquois model, nine metres long and eight metres wide, with two Mercedes outboard engines to use if there was no wind for the sails. After formalities, training, practice manoeuvrings, fueling, stocking up at the ship chandler and a tour of two supermarkets, they set sail at eight o'clock to arrive in the port of Saint-Florent on the northeast coast of the Corsican Island around five o'clock in the morning on Sunday, the following day.

Sally was a great cook and made even the most gastronomical dishes look easy to prepare. She appointed herself 'chief cook and bottle washer'. The galley was compact and functional. They prepared a big salad with everything in it except the kitchen sink, opened some beers and ate outdoors on the deck while leaving the Cote d'Azur landscape far behind. No noise, just the sound of the waves and the wind in their hair and sails. Anthony had put up the spinnaker taking advantage of the backwind to get them across the Mediterranean Sea to Corsica quicker.

Glancing at Anthony's profile as the rays of the sun shone on his face while sinking below the horizon, Lili thought he looked particularly handsome and noble. He was happy to be on the catamaran and sailing, especially to Corsica, the island he knew and loved so well and especially to leave work and his demons behind. He told them to get some kip; he would ring the ship's bell if there was any imminent danger or if he needed help or some company.

At three o'clock, Lili went up on the deck with mugs of hot tea. She had slept for three hours and was feeling on top of the world. Unlike Anthony, who was dog-tired, he told her to steer and keep the cap on the direction of the compass he pointed to. They were scheduled to hit dry land in under three hours, and he wanted to take a short nap.

This is paradise, she thought; *no madden crowd or traffic din, only stars shining brightly up above, the soft breeze, the smell of the iodine sea with nothing in sight*. After two hours of absolute solitary bliss, Sally and James, followed by Anthony, came on deck just as she spotted the outline of Corsica. "Land ahoy", she laughed while looking through her binoculars.

Out of nowhere, dolphins started to race beside the catamaran, and one jumped completely over the starboard to the port side. There were at least ten swimming in the same direction keeping close to the side of the catamaran and accompanying them. Anthony was smiling and saying they often did that during the early morning hours to get something to eat. This time they were unlucky; they got nought because there was nothing suitable on board to give them. They made a pledge to get food to be able to throw in the sea to them on their next supermarket spree. Lili photographed the splendid mammals in action, frolicking and swimming in the amazing sunrise light.

The four of them were over-excited, moving on adrenalin sailing into the port of Saint-Florent in the early morning mist.

"The last one to jump a shore will pay for le *petit-déjeuner* – breakfast," shouted Anthony jovially.

They were thankful the crossing had passed without incident; they had taken the sails down and were motoring in slowly toward the Capitainerie – the harbour master's office – to register, pay the tax and get instructions where to moor the vessel in the port.

A few days passed, and they were really enjoying Corsica and well into the holiday mood. They had already visited other ports and a couple of white sandy beaches with warm turquoise azure-coloured waters.

"What shall we do with the drunken sailor, what shall we do with the drunken sailor, what shall we do with the drunken sailor early in the mornin'?"

James was singing at the top of his voice on the windsurfer gliding over to the beach with their picnic in his backpack.

"God help our bellies if he falls in the sea, we'll have no bloody lunch," Sally swore, "Was it really a good idea to bring those two windsurf boards?" Sally screeched to Lili.

"You bet they're great fun; we can race one another and get onto beaches with them without having to risk anchoring too close because the engines may get stuck in the sandbanks. They're useful, just like the folding tandem bikes we brought to get us around on land when we're in ports or doing tourist-type things. You can't say we didn't think of everything, and they were so cheap to rent, well, compared to the price of the catamaran rental anyway."

A few nights later, after eating a typical Corsican meal of Cabrettu, a type of pork stew, and as a starter, some thin slices of hams: la Coppa, le Lonzu, le Prisuttu and le Figatellu at an authentic local restaurant near the harbour in Ajaccio, Anthony wanted to set sail to get to the town of Bonifacio further south, on the peak of the island, that is situated just twelve kilometres north of the bigger island of Sardinia, by the morning. He had not checked the weather forecast, which was totally insane. He thought it was going to be a good night's sail due to the day's good weather, which had been very hot, dry and sunny with a gentle breeze. However, everyone knows the Mediterranean Sea can be very treacherous and unpredictable.

"We're right out to sea now; we can barely make out the coastline. As Captain, I've mapped the route. Go and get some sleep, you three, and I'll wake Lili up around two forty-five to take the next watch. We should all be on deck around six o'clock to witness the amazing sight of sailing into the Bonifacio port through the gigantic narrow, grey rock channel."

Anthony was tired when he swapped watches with Lili after waking her. She drank a mug of hot herbal tea, telling him she had set the alarm and would wake him up later. It had turned into a dark, cold starless night. Lili settled onto the captain's seat at the helm. She was feeling uneasy and realised how far they were from the coast. She could see lightning ahead in the far distance as the catamaran was gliding through the sea. Soon, the wind was blowing hard, and she heard thunder. Suddenly the gusts of wind in the sails were making the catamaran go very fast, aqua planning, not even touching the water. Then thuds as the two hulls hit the sea again. She tried to hold the bar steady; she was scared. Anthony, Sally and James hurried on deck as the pots, pans and untied crockery were breaking and falling below in the galley during the storm that was breaking, and just as the mizzen mast broke in half, trailing the sail in the rough sea.

"Merde, merde, merde, Lili, I'll take over, hang on tightly; we're in for a very rough sail. Put your safety jackets on. It's all my fault; I'm the only one to blame. I should have checked the weather forecast before we left Ajaccio. What a fool, a stupid fool. *Bordel de merde.* Let's get you harnessed so that you can crawl forward on all fours and bring the sail back onto the catamaran; you're the only one who can do it because you're the shortest and probably the fittest. We'll hold your lines firmly, don't worry, get going, hurry up."

Anthony looked afraid and angry with himself. Lili did as she was told and was petrified, crawling forward over the net between the hulls bringing in the sail bit by bit and what seemed to her to be inch by inch and interminable. The wind howled around her ears, and the waves completely soaked her. Though freezing, she managed to get the job done. Anthony made radio contact with the Bonifacio lighthouse keeper, Captain Marcel. He was able to give him their position and guided them safely to Bonifacio, where they navigated through the rock channel with high cliffs on both sides several hours later. Captain Marcel was waving his hat at them from way above on the clifftops. Plans were made for the mast to be repaired. Sometime later, they bought the biggest and finest bottle of Courvoisier VSOP for Captain Marcel and helped him drink some of the fine cognacs while thanking him and raising their caps and hats. They had experienced a bad-trip adventure to tell their friends and anyone else who would listen when they got back to Paris.

An adventure that Lili would have preferred to do without, but she had miraculously lived to tell the tale, and Anthony was proud of her, for once.

Of course, that incident spoiled the remainder of the holiday, but they did do all the visits they had planned, including going from Corsica to the Italian Riviera on the return journey via the east coast of Corsica, starting at the town of Alessio and following the coast all the way back to the French Riviera to Port Grimaud to return the rented catamaran.

Lili noticed throughout the following weeks and months a definite turn for the worse in Anthony's behaviour. She was angry with Paul for not keeping in touch with Anthony or with her, for that matter. Anthony had no appetite and was even more withdrawn and moody. He chain-smoked while coughing profusely. He finally agreed to see a doctor who diagnosed a psycho-sematic nervous illness and prescribed some mild tranquillizers, and told him to practice some sports to take his mind off work and whatever else it was that caused him distress.

They tried to go more often to play archery on weekends to Anthony's Godfather's house, just an hour and a half's drive from home. It certainly helped Lili to relax and took Anthony's mind off things. He loved discussing politics with his now-retired Godfather when the latter was not working in his vegetable garden.

Lili had started temping in the Headquarters of an American conglomerate in the heart of Paris. She had a six-month renewable contract to create a completely new dynamic filing system, as the current one in the big department was obsolete due to new procedures. The work was as boring as hell, but she loved the international environment and her colleagues. The after-work parties were great fun, and she soon found herself with a large circle of friends from all corners of the world, as well as her existing friends and family-in-law. All was fine, except that Anthony was jealous of her new life and job. He did not want her to go out, but he did not want to join them either.

Lili had been living in France for five years when things got very much worse with Anthony's mental health. One day he told her he wanted to buy a flat just outside Paris instead of renting a place. Lili immediately agreed; being a homeowner instead of a tenant was much better and a good investment for the future. The mortgage interest rates were attractive at that point in time, so they made the decision to do it, move out of Paris to the suburbs. They spent long evenings looking through the property markets, visiting real-estate agencies and properties during weekends. Autumn was approaching, and with it, the dark nights. Flat hunting gave them a common interest. Lili was going to be unable to go out as often with her new friends. That pleased Anthony; his idea of getting away from the centre of Paris was also to get her back for himself as it was going to be longer and more difficult to travel home on public transport in the evenings.

Six months later, they signed at the Solicitor for a two-bedroom flat that had a big terrace where they could put garden furniture and eat under the branches of a big oak tree on the top floor of a seven-storey, ten-year-old apartment building west of Paris overlooking the Seine River. Lili was in her element decorating and furnishing, but Anthony hated it; he loathed it. He was kicking himself about his idea to move out of Paris. Lili was busy all the time choosing paint, and curtains, looking at colour schemes and getting quotes from kitchen and bathroom fitters.

Anthony was continuing to take his medication, and besides practising archery, he and Lili went running on the track along the river some evenings after work and during weekends. One early evening he fell and could not catch his breath. Lili got the car and drove him to the emergency unit at the nearest hospital. He was diagnosed with a slight heart complaint and was told to give up smoking immediately. He was given a new treatment to take on top of the existing one and was advised to get in touch with a cardiologist, which he did not.

One night when Lili was returning home late from work, she took a hired car that was paid for by the company for women employees who worked after eight o'clock. She had a deadline for the enormous filing system to be totally complete. It had taken her six months, and she had practically finished. Her boss wanted to put her on a new assignment, but on one condition only, that she became a full-time employee of the firm instead of a temp. She needed to think the offer over carefully because she was not sure she wanted to stay married to Anthony and remain in the Paris area. She had married him for better or worse, but where she was at now, after only six years of marriage, seemed very much for the worse. Staying together seemed impossible as they had become incompatible in every way. She was moving in one direction, and he in another.

Lili enjoyed the ride in the black Mercedes and the conversation with the chauffeur during the forty-minute drive home. He was very witty, and she acknowledged he was well-dressed, suave, charming, and interesting. When he got out of the car to open the door, she was surprised to see such a gleam in his dark green eyes. They shook hands, a handshake that she couldn't stop thinking about. After leaving the chauffeur and opening the front door to find Anthony in the dark, sleeping on the sofa with the television on but no sound, she turned on the lights, woke him up, and began preparing the evening meal. She was ravenous after a hard day's work.

Paul had been back in Paris from his assignment in Washington, DC, for a while. He had brought Kate back with him. Lili and Anthony were witnesses at their civil wedding at the Town Hall in Paris and attended the religious wedding followed by a gigantic feast in a beautiful all-white marquee on Kate's parents' property in the countryside on a very hot summer's day in July.

Anthony rarely spoke to them now and never accepted their invitations to any event. He was so jealous of Kate and made no effort to hide it. He said only rude things about her behind her back, which was unfair because she was very attractive, intelligent, and witty. That was probably why he didn't like her. Lili became friends with Kate, and they sometimes met for lunch in Paris and phoned each other from their offices. Lili confided and shared her doubts about what she thought was Anthony's true feelings towards Paul. In the beginning, Kate was sceptical and utterly surprised. But as time went by, she said she could see the matter was serious but was unable to talk to Paul about it. Kate herself suffered from continuous reprimands from Paul's mother, who thought she was not good enough for her son and didn't take enough care of him. Kate was an emancipated educated young woman who believed in task sharing at home and equality for the sexes. She and her mother-in-law were from different generations. Kate was the type that thought if your glass was half empty, add some vodka!

Out of the blue one evening, while getting off at the bus stop in front of her apartment building, Lili saw the black Mercedes that had brought her home a few weeks prior parked in her courtyard. The chauffeur stepped out immediately as she walked past, and he greeted her with *Bonsoir Mademoiselle* – Good evening, Miss. Lili returned his smile, saying she was madame. They chatted for a few minutes. She asked if he had come to her address to meet a passenger. He had not; he had dropped off a client nearby and said he was waiting for her. He could not see the lights on in her flat, and he had no more clients to chauffeur that evening. He wanted to invite her for a drink. She wondered how he knew which apartment was hers. He explained he always waited until women passengers entered their homes at night and turned on the lights before he drove off, thus ensuring there were no bad incidents. He had seen the lights go on in Lili's apartment when he had dropped her off. It was written in his contract with her employer. He was a private chauffeur with his own business and clients.

Lili was flattered by the invitation but said her husband was waiting for her. This was not the truth. Anthony was now working away from home, mostly in the northeast of France, three nights a week, as a consultant to companies who required new system integration or updates to their current computer systems. This was part of his new job at the firm he had worked for, for the past twelve years. He hated it and hated having to sleep in hotels and not at home.

The chauffeur introduced himself as Julien Petit; he already knew her name. He said he might pass by again another time in case she changed her mind, then said *Bonne nuit* – Goodnight.

Chapter Eleven

BREAKING UP ISN'T EASY

Her decision was made about Anthony. She had come to it, though it had been a hand-wringing experience more than a week ago. The hardest part about Lili making a decision, no matter what the situation or circumstances, was always her indecisiveness and incapacity to remove her feelings from the equation and just look and measure the hard facts and reality. Once she had done that, and her decision was made, she stuck to it and never looked back, even if it hurt.

Lili decided to divorce Anthony and rent a furnished flat on the Avenue de l'Opera, a few minutes' walk to the famous Parisian Opera House, known as the Palais Garnier – Garnier Palace- opened in 1875, after building began in 1861, by the architect Charles Garnier, in the New-Baroque style of the Second Empire, with a seating capacity of around 1900. Lili loved the ostentatious building and also liked to have a drink in the evening or tea in the afternoons during the weekends in the Café de La Paix next door to it on the corner of boulevard des Capucines and the Place de l'Opéra.

The large bright flat was owned by one of her friends who was leaving Paris for a year's tour to visit relatives and friends in Australia. That gave her enough time to file for divorce and try one last time to make Anthony admit to himself, once and for all, that he was not paranoid but had feelings for men, not women. There was nothing wrong with that. He had to stop making himself ill he must seek specialised medical help and go into therapy. He was not in love with her, and she could not stand the situation any longer. She was suffering; they had been living a lie, performing, keeping up appearances and pretending. Enough was enough.

Before taking her final decision, she had spoken over the phone on several occasions to her mother, Elsa-May, her sister, Ivy, and of course to cousin Jen. She also tried, but had somehow not succeeded, in talking to Anthony's youngest brother, Jonathan and his wife, Claire. In truth, she was in a very unhappy and difficult situation, in a relationship that she was no longer able to bear. She wanted to have a child and be a mother, but not with Anthony. Lili knew that he had become a stranger. She still wanted to be in love with Anthony, her husband, but she was not; he had made life for them together impossible.

Lili had taken entrance exams and passed two interviews to become a full-time member of staff, a regular employee, not just a temp. Her boss, a Vice-President, was delighted.

She was to become his right arm, delegate projects to her, and work that she could handle on an everyday basis to free him to get the three-year and five-year business plans ready for the firm to operate in sensitive-political places around the globe that needed high-tech to propel them for a move into the twenty-first century. She was to take the initiative and, bring all ideas forward, think out of the box. These were her objectives and challenges. Lili was organised, trustworthy, dedicated and was going to be able to meet those objectives as his Personal Assistant. On top of that, she loved challenges. With her new marital status, it would keep her time and mind occupied instead of dwelling on past failures. She thought of her divorce as a personal failure and was harsh on herself.

The show-down with Anthony was hard on them both that Saturday when she moved herself and her personal belongings out of their home, but only after he agreed to write and sign a paper giving her his permission to leave their home. Otherwise, she would be accused of desertion and lose her rights to any divorce compensation. Not that she was interested in material things or money; she wanted her freedom. The right to live in peace and harmony, to do and go where she pleased, if and when it pleased her.

Chapter Twelve

A NEW BEGINNING

One evening, well into summer, after leaving the office late from the main reception entrance, Lili saw Julien Petit, the chauffeur, standing in front of his car, obviously waiting for one of the executives. They said hello and past the time of day. He told her he was going to drive one of the vice-presidents to a restaurant on the Avenue des Champs-Elysées and would be free in less than twenty minutes, and if she was hungry, they could eat together. As it happened, Lili had no other plans and had not felt like going home to her empty flat near the Opera alone and was glad of the chance to have dinner with Julien Petit. He gave her the name and address of a bistro he knew that was pleasant and within walking distance; he would meet her there.

Lili had rarely spent such a good evening completely off-the-cuff; those types of evenings usually turned out to be the best ones, totally unplanned. She laughed until tears fell down her face because Julien was a very entertaining man full of self-derision and told funny stories about everything under the sun and about clients he'd driven in his car or to places he had visited. She was relaxed, and time flew by.

Julien Petit was recently divorced and had a nine-year-old daughter called Adèle. He had custody of her three days and nights a week and half of the school holidays. On 'his' days, he only worked until he met her after school. On the other days and nights, he worked long hours to compensate for the loss of income. Julien was devoted to his daughter and was hurting after his divorce from Adèle's mother, a wife who had left him for another man. Lili listened attentively and compassionately about his life as a father and could tell it was going to take him a long time to get over the deception.

Lili told him how much she wanted a child and about her divorce, which was in the final stage. She and Anthony had met with the judge, together with their respective lawyers, to see if reconciliation was possible, but it was not. Lili didn't want her old life back. Anthony had decided to leave the Paris region and return to his hometown in the Alps, at least for a year. He didn't need to earn big money. He only required a simple life skiing in the winter and playing tennis or practising archery in the summer. He had many family members scattered about in the region, as well as some good old friends. His firm had agreed to him taking a year's sabbatical leave, and he was going to seek medical help for the way he was feeling.

After their off-the-cuff dinner, Julien Petit drove Lili to the entrance of her apartment building and promptly asked for her phone number. He suggested they drive out with Adèle during the following weekend to have a picnic and play some games or frisbee or whatever they fancied. Lili was delighted and quickly agreed. As much as Lili loved to go to fancy restaurants, especially the best ones that had gourmet-stars and rave reviews, she loved to picnic just as much. She told him if they did go, not to do anything about the food as she would get everything ready and bring it in a wicker picnic basket. His only task was to drive them to a lovely place where they could lay it all out on a gingham tablecloth.

Lili was unprepared for the way she felt when she first met Adèle. Adèle was a pretty little nine-year-old girl, brown-eyed, olive-skinned, with long dark hair. Her two front teeth were missing and had dimples at each side of her mouth whenever she smiled, and she smiled and laughed all the time, mischief written all over her forehead. She chuckled as she teased her father at every available opportunity. Julien Petit loved it; he loved his daughter and loved being with her. He always said she was the one good thing that came out of his broken marriage, and she saved him from wallowing in self-pity.

So, this is what it's like, Lili thought, imagining herself as a mother. *To be a mother, it's not essential to be a biological one; loving a child and raising that child to become a fine human being can be as good as it gets.* Lili loved Adèle the moment she set eyes on her; it was a simple truth.

While listening to the radio, playing cassettes and singing to Dire Straits, Phil Collins and Lionel Richie, Julien drove them for over an hour on the A13 Motorway west of Paris to the medieval town of Gisors in the department of Eure in the Normandy region.

Gisors is some forty kilometres from Auvers-sur-Oise, where the brothers Vincent and Theo van Gogh are buried next to each other in the cemetery on the outskirts of the beautiful town. Julien said they would go there on their next picnic. He was bantering with both Lili and Adèle. He looked relaxed, as did Lili. She had only seen him wearing business suits and ties; today, he was dressed casually smart wearing blue cotton Bermuda shorts and a matching Lacoste shirt. He took her hand.

They laid her gingham tablecloth on the green grass on the left bank of the river Epte. The church clock was striking one o'clock, and Lili's stomach thought her throat had been cut; she was famished. She had woken up very early and drank a pot of tea before seven o'clock but had been unable to eat; she was feeling nervous. She did not know why; she just was. The smell of the flowers and the grass was sweet in her nostrils. She realised it had been a long time since she had gone out of Paris. She was relaxing while serving the cold roast chicken, ham slices, potato salad, and houmous with pita bread, strawberries and watermelon. The rosé wine was in the cooler that Julien had already opened to be served in the crystal glasses.

He made a toast to Lili for the great picnic and organisation. Adèle said "chin-chin" - cheers - with her canned pineapple juice and hugged her dad.

As time passed, Julien phoned Lili during the day in her office and in the evenings. Before hanging up, he always fixed a date for their next meeting. He was very serious about Lili; he told her Adèle was always asking about her and where and when they would next meet. Weekends away with him and Adèle and barbecues in the garden were her only activities. She was neglecting her friends; tongues were wagging.

It was inevitable and happened naturally; they became lovers, and Lili felt happy for the first time in her long memory. She was sure of her feelings and was truly in love with Julien and adored Adèle.

Chapter Thirteen

LIFE BEGINS AT THIRTY

On the day of her thirtieth birthday in October, Lili moved into Julien's house, and it fell on a Saturday. Although it was not one of the weekends Adèle was supposed to be with her father, she was there any way to help with the move. She was jumping around, especially on the new bed they had bought, and carrying items up the steps into the house. Adèle was so happy and delighted to know that when she was with her father in the house, the three of them would be together. Her parents' divorce had been hard on Adèle as an only child. Lili knew she must make a special effort to reassure Adèle and let her know she was not just a woman who was here today and gone tomorrow. It was not difficult because Lili had every intention of never going away.

They drove over to England, taking the car ferry at Christmas for Lili to introduce Julien and Adèle to her family in Chester. All the presents were packed in the boot of Julien's personal white diesel-engine Cadillac. He loved American cars; it was not one of the cars he used for clients. Adèle was excited to spend Christmas in a foreign country where they spoke a different language. She tried to imitate the people they met and always giggled.

They stopped to fill the tank at the Service Station at the entrance to the M1 Motorway that would take them up North on that Christmas Eve afternoon. Lili wanted to do it, but Julien told her to take Adèle to the toilet and get some sweets and sandwiches. The five-hour drive was going to be very long for her, and he hoped she would sleep during part of the journey.

One mile up the motorway, the car engine started spluttering, and the car came to a complete standstill in the middle lane of the motorway. It had started snowing, and there were at least a hundred cars piled up behind them, full of people going up North from London to spend Christmas with their families. The sound of car horns shrieking at them was unbearable. They could not push the car to the side because it had an automatic gearbox, and nothing worked, not even the steering wheel. Julien figured out that by mistake, he had put unleaded petrol instead of diesel fuel in the tank, and until they got the gallons of it out of the tank, the car was not going to budge.

Suddenly, from out of nowhere, lights flashing, a motorway rescue truck came alongside them and got the gist of the problem. The driver hooked their car onto the rescue platform and drove them to the car park of the nearest garage off the motorway, but it was closing for four days during the holiday period, the same as all the other garages.

"Mon Dieu – My God! What the hell are we going to do? Let me use your phone to call my sister, she's in the Police Force and will definitely have a solution to our problem, if she doesn't, nobody will.

Hi, Ivy; it's me, Lili. I'm calling from a garage we've broken down on the M1 motorway and are not going to be able to get to Chester because all the garages are closed or closing. If you cannot help us, we will need to stay in a hotel if we can find one that's open. Can you help us? Yes, you can, that's great, all right, I can give you the address of this garage and phone number. Please call me back as soon as you can."

The mechanic at the garage got irate; he wanted to go home before the big snowstorm started; he should have closed hours ago. However, ten minutes later, his phone rang, and he handed it to Lili; it was Ivy.

"OK, listen, I've phoned the Automobile Association of which I'm a member, you know, the AA. Well, they will send a breakdown vehicle to that garage where you are, and it will put your car on the trailer and drive it and the three of you up to Chester. Don't worry; the whole thing will be paid for by my insurance, and the rescue truck will be there within the hour. See you later; everything's going to be fine, don't panic. We'll wait for you to eat dinner together. Mum has got the snails and the horsemeat steaks sorted!"

Ivy was so clever and funny. Little Adèle was in her element, sitting in the cabin of the rescue truck, drawing snowmen on the steamed-up windows. Julien felt like a complete idiot, and Lili was laughing at the absurdity of the situation. She told Julien he had done it on purpose so that he didn't have to drive on the left side of the road. He kissed her and told her how much he loved her; he really did. He was very emotional; he was French.

Chapter Fourteen

THE MISSING ELEMENT

While drinking their pre-lunch drinks in the living room after returning from the pub, traditionally at three o'clock on Christmas day, the smell of the roast stuffed turkey and the trimmings floated through the whole house. Elsa-May standing at the stove, looked as happy as Larry and couldn't stop smiling like a Cheshire cat who was licking cream off its whiskers. She and Julien hit it off straight away when they arrived the previous night. They found they had a lot in common; his daughter, Adèle, was the cherry on the cake.

"Let's open all the gifts now before we carve the turkey and begin our Christmas lunch. Our Ivy must go on duty at seven o'clock, and we don't want to rush our Christmas food, do we?"

As the youngest person in the group, Adèle went to the beautifully decorated Christmas tree and read the names on the gift-wrapped packages and distributed them appropriately to Elsa-May, Ivy, Lee, Rod, their wives, Julien and Lili. She kept the six packages on which her name was written.

One of Lili's presents was in a huge package; she had never seen one so big. She already wondered what it was when she saw Julien secretly putting it in the car boot when they left the house on their journey. They all began unwrapping their presents, some were ones they needed and wanted, and some were frivolous.

Lili had started unwrapping the big one, but every time she ripped one layer off, there was another smaller wrapped box inside. A wrapped box in a wrapped box, this went on eight times, and everyone was laughing, highly amused, until Lili finally came to the present, a small silver-coloured metal swan.

"Oh, a silver-coloured metal swan; it's very cute and original. All that for this, thank you, Julien."

"You must open the swan; it's in two parts. Look closer."

When she opened the swan, she found a tiny box inside containing an exquisite white gold ring with a solitary diamond that looked like an engagement ring. She thought about what her gran used to say, that good things come in small parcels, and she grinned.

Lili was so flabbergasted and found it hard to speak. Tears welled up in her eyes; she started to shake while gazing in disbelief at the unique and soberly beautiful solitary diamond ring. No man had ever been so romantic towards her; she was overwhelmed with happiness.

Julien went and sat on the floor beside her and took her in his arms. He asked if she would marry him and let him place the ring on her engagement finger. The family didn't understand the French conversation, only the gist of the scene, but they did understand that Lili must answer an important question quickly before they could eat the Christmas lunch; they were starving.

"But Julien, we've never spoken about marriage, only that I should show Adèle that I will be a permanent figure in her life and not go away or leave her like her biological mother. At the same time, I've grown to love you deeper every day, with every gest you make and all the things you do. After all, it's not what you say that's important; it's what you do on a daily basis that shows the depth of love and feelings. When my divorce from Anthony became final, and I held the decree absolute in my hand, I said, "never again". I felt because of my divorce I was a failure, as if I had a flaw, like I had done something terribly wrong. But today, I'm ready to take a chance with you, ready to say "yes." Yes, because it feels right. I no longer need to ruminate over the past and ask myself questions about the future. I believe the missing element in my life has been a child. Now with

Adèle, there is no missing element. The three of us are together. The long and winding road led me to your door."

Chapter Fifteen

AN ODE TO ELSA-MAY

There once was a lass from Liverpool

Born too early, she nearly died at birth during that terrible stormy night

They named her Elsa-May, weighing just over two pounds on that June night.

She became strong, willful, brave, loyal, loving and giving.

Searching that which would be her mission in this life.

At the age of eighteen, she went off to war, WW2.

She realised that justice must be done

Hitler could not and would not win.

Caring as a nurse for others and learning the meaning of it all.

Still searching that which would be her mission in this life.

Daughter, sister, cousin, friend, lover, pianist and dancer,

she played all those roles so well.

A Connie Millington dancing team girl.

Dancing in a ballroom in Liverpool on a Saturday night.

Resting at the bar, blushing while standing close to LJ,

That handsome Irish heroic soldier, back from the trip to hell.

"What's your name," he asked

"Elsa-May," came the reply.

"Elsa-May I'll marry you before the year is out."

Searching no more, that which would be her mission in this life.

Mother of four bonnie children, to her were born.

On that road of the mission in her life.

Nana of ten toddlers, who subsequently came along,

On the path of her mission in this life.

The good die young, Elsa-May no exception to the rule,

God bless her beloved soul, now resting in peace,

After accomplishing her mission in this life.

Elsa-May, watching over her fold from afar, from the invisible,

Whispering - Let there be love between them.

Never let it be forgotten that family love is the greatest gift of all

Bringing sense to her life's mission

Index Of The Main Characters

Adam – Flavie's husband and Anthony's friend

Adèle – Julien Petit's daughter

Annabelle – Anthony's sister-in-law

Anthony – Lili's French husband

Betty – Lili's colleague in London

Cassandra – Lili's employer and owner of the perfumery

Chas – Gran's lover

Claire – Anthony's sister-in-law

Dan – Lili's London flatmate

Deidra – LJ's lover

Dominique – Lili's friend and gynaecologist in Paris

Dotty / Dorothy – Jen's mother and Lili's auntie

Elsa-May – Lili's mother

Flavie – Anthony's friend and wife of Adam in Paris

Jen – Lili's cousin, Dotty's daughter & Stan's sister

Jonathan – Anthony's younger brother

Julien Petit – Chauffeur, Adèle's father & Lili's French boyfriend

Gran – Lili's maternal grandmother

Igor – One of Lili's bosses in London and Antony's Best Man

James – Lili's English friend in Paris & catamaran crew

Jay – Lili's first love boyfriend and Pygmalion

Ivy – Lili's younger sister

Kate – Paul's French wife

Lee – Lili's eldest brother

Madame Beaumont – Anthony's mother

Madame Moreau – Lili's French teacher at the Alliance Française

Mademoiselle Mercier – Lili's French teacher at the Sorbonne open university

Monsieur Beaumont – Anthony's father

Olivia – Igor's wife and Lili's friend in London

Paige – Lili's English Sorbonne open university friend

Patrick – Anthony's eldest brother

Paul – Anthony's French friend

Pauline – Lili's friend from London

Pete – Jen's first boyfriend in Liverpool

Reg – Pauline's husband from London

Rob – Lili's boss in London

Rod – Lili's youngest brother

Sally – Lili's English friend in Paris, catamaran crew

Sarah – Stan's Australian nurse and partner

Sofia – Paige's sister and PA to Cassandra

Stan – Jen's brother, Dotty's son & Lili's cousin in Australia

Lightning Source UK Ltd.
Milton Keynes UK
UKHW020903271222
414464UK00014B/795